I MISS MY PROJECTS

Y. BLAK MOORE

ALSO BY Y. BLAK MOORE

DEDICATION

I dedicate this one to my brother,
Willie Coker the Ghost Rider a.k.a. Rat,
a prince of the projects.
Rest In Power.
Word

First printing: 2020
ISBN 9781734907032
R & M Publications
Chicago, Illinois 60628

Ordering information:
Special discounts are available on quantity purchases by corporations, associations, educators, and others. For details contact the publisher.

U.S. trade bookstores and wholesalers, please contact:
R & M Publications
Tel: (773)650-9720 or rhuemoorebooks@gmail.com
www.yblakmoore.com

ONCE UPON A TIME IN THE PROJECTS...

CHAPTER ONE

Monroe "Roe" Pearson stood in the back hallway of a row house in the Martin Luther King Houses housing project, separating and counting the handful of money he'd just made. His black Wing-Ding hat was cocked to the right, atop his braids that seriously needed to be washed and re-braided. When he was through counting, he peeked his head out of the hallway and looked at Paul "Polo" French Jr., sitting on the iron railing of the porch.

"Polo, waddup Family, how long?" Roe asked, as he took a rubber band off of his wrist and wrapped it around the knot of money.

Polo looked up from his two-way pager and hunched his shoulders. "Hold on," he said. "Yo L.J., how long, fool?"

Leon "L.J." Jones and Carlos "Cuckoo Carl" Smith were across the courtyard perched on some milk crates, resting their backs on the cool bricks of the row house wall behind them. L.J. was playing with a toothpick at the corner of his mouth, and Cuckoo was picking up small rocks from the ground, throwing them at the crack customers loitering in the courtyard.

"We waitin' on Big Tee fat ass," L.J. called out. "He said 10 minutes like 20 minutes ago. I'm calling his Startec, but the fat fuck ain't answerin'. I'm 'bout to page him 911 in a minute."

Polo called out to the crackheads in the back courtyard, "Ten minutes, mothafuckas! Have yo money ready, because we ain't finta be playin' wit yo ass!"

Several of the waiting customers grumbled because they'd

been waiting longer than 10 minutes already. One of the braver addicts approached L.J. and Cuckoo Carl. He was a dark skin, bald head man with a wide nose and scruffy beard. Though it was a cool, autumn day with an overcast sky, the man was sweating. The two boys could easily smell the funkiness wafting from the man's filthy sweatshirt and pants.

"No disrespect, boss," he said. "but you niggas been said ten minutes like two, three times. I don't wanna go nowhere else because y'all be having the best ready-rocks, but I ain't got all day."

Cuckoo sat forward on his milk crate and pulled his gun out and sat it on his lap. He said, "Who the fuck you think you talkin' to, mufucka? If you don't get yo musty ass the fuck away from this porch, you 'bout to be wearin' a shitbag for the rest of yo life."

L.J. put his hand on Cuckoo's arm. He ordered, "Put that up. It's too early in the morning to be shootin' a nigga over shit." To the crackhead, he said, "Look nigga, if we say ten minutes and it take ten hours, oh well. Either wait or don't, but to show you that we men of our word, if the shop ain't back open in ten minutes, then everybody's first crack is on us."

The look of fear from almost being shot seconds ago was replaced by a look of joy on the crack addict's face. He wiped his sweaty forehead with the back of his hand. "Hell yeah! That's what I'm talkin' about. That's why I fucks with you Family niggas like this. Y'all can always get my money. I'm countin' down too, so don't be on no bullshit."

"Yeah, well count the fuck somewhere else nigga," Cuckoo said, as he returned his pistol to the back of his pants.

The man walked back over to the parking lot and sat on the hood of a rusted out Delta 88 parked there. They could actually hear him counting, "One Mississippi, two Mississippi, three Mississippi..."

"L.J., how the fuck you gone give away crack?" asked Polo. He had walked over to them. "That shit ain't free."

"Oh, it ain't gone be free," L.J. assured him. "Ain't shit free in life, but them sammiches from the choke house. That fat ass nigga, Big Tee, gotta learn that he can't be bullshittin' with the work. I don't know no better way than to give away

3

some ready-rocks and take them out his pay. Call his fat ass again, Polo."

Polo took his Motorola cell phone from the clip on his belt and dialed Big Tee's number. Big Tee answered. Polo said, "Boy, where yo' fat ass at? We got customers like a mufucka out here. Okay, keep bullshitting with the bundles. We tellin' the cluckers if you not here in ten minutes their first rock is free, and the shit is coming out yo' pay. So gone head keep fuckin' around. I know yo' freaky ass ain't doing shit but getting yo' dick sucked or eatin' or both. You betta come on, you only got like six minutes left."

Polo hung up and returned his phone to the clip. "His fat ass ain't doing nothin' but trickin' off. All that nigga do is buy food, shoes and pussy, I swear."

"He shole keep Ericka little, bald head ass in some fresh K-Swiss, tho," L.J. said with a laugh.

"He need to buy that bitch some bangs," Cuckoo added. "Or some sideburns with her small head ass."

As they were laughing at Cuckoo's comment, there was a commotion as Terrell "Big Tee" Princeton hurried into the courtyard. He was walking as fast as his fat legs would carry him, with the fly of his pants unzipped. He wore a leather Troop jacket with a matching pair of Troop gym shoes. The crack users in the back courtyard recognized him immediately and knew he was there with a fresh supply of crack, destroying their hopes of receiving a free dime bag.

"Speaking of the devil, here go his fat ass now," L.J. said.

Big Tee walked over to them and shook each of their hands with their clique's handshake.

"Fuck yo' fat ass been, G?" Cuckoo asked.

"Somewhere stretchin' some smoker's jaws, I bet," L.J. commented.

"Man, I wasn't on nothin'," Big Tee replied. "I was chillin'."

"Yeah, right," Cuckoo added. "Well why yo' pants unzipped, Mr. I Was Chilling?"

Bashfully, Big Tee zipped his Levi's. "Man, that don't mean nothin'. I'm tellin' you, I smoked two joints and ate a steak sub at Cindy Brady crib and I fell asleep."

As they talked, a pre-teen boy rode a brand-new Mongoose BMX style bicycle with mag wheels into the backyard. There was a girl about the same age wearing a new pair of Reebok Pump shoes, standing on the stunt pegs of the bike. Her hands were on the boy's shoulders as he steered and she was wearing a bookbag on her back. The girl on the back of the bike, Sakenah "Squeak" Thomas, locked eyes with Big Tee. With a nod of his head, Big Tee directed them over to the hallway where Roe was waiting. The pair rode over to the hallway. Squeak jumped off the back of the bike and darted inside the hallway while Polo walked back over and took his place on the porch again. Inside the hallway, Squeak turned her back to Roe. He quickly unzipped the backpack and took the large Ziploc freezer storage bag full of dime bags of crack out of it. He dropped the knot of money he'd made from the previous bundle into the backpack and zipped it back up. He unzipped the baggie and pulled out a handful of crack bags.

"Awight, Squeak, tell Polo I'm ready, shorty," Roe said.

Out on the porch, Squeak walked past Polo and jumped down onto the stunt pegs of her chauffeur's bike. "He reloaded," Squeak told him as she tapped the boy's shoulder on the bike seat, letting him know to ride away.

Polo surveyed the customers milling around and he walked over to stand by the hallway door. "Roe, you got a real crowd out here," he said. "I'll collect money for you, you just serve 'til we get rid of this rush. You ready?"

Roe nodded. Polo proclaimed, "We workin'! We workin'! Big bags! Butter on the crack! Ready-rocks! Ready-rocks! Get y'all ass in line!"

Instantly, the crackheads rushed to form a line over by the hallway. They were pushing one another and jostling each other to get a better position in line, so Cuckoo Carl left his milk crate seat and walked over to the crowd.

"Y'all, better calm the fuck down before don't nobody be gettin' shit!" he threatened. "I ain't tellin' you mufuckas nothin' but one time neither."

The customers settled down and started to step up onto the porch one at a time. As each one reached his or her turn, they would pay Polo for their purchase and step into the hallway to receive their product. The line advanced along in an orderly fashion. Soon it was the addict's turn that L.J. promised the free crack if the shop wasn't open in ten minutes.

To Polo, he said, "By my count that was 12 minutes and yo' mans said we get a free one after ten minutes."

"Move to the side," Polo ordered as he continued to collect money and send customers in the hallway. "You really think you 'bout to get some free yams, nigga? You can't be fuckin' serious. Where yo' watch at nigga since you clockin' shit?"

"I ain't got no watch, if I did I would have sold it to y'all by now," the crackhead explained. "I'm tellin' y'all I was countin'. It's been 12 minutes by my count, too."

"You know how stupid you sound, Joe?" Polo asked. "Look, do you want to buy or not? If not, move yo' ass around. Somebody else workin', go to the buildings or the walk-ups, but get the fuck from back here."

Sensing he couldn't win, the crackhead handed over his ten bucks and went in the hallway to collect his one lonely bag.

Seeing that the line was orderly and flowing smooth, Cuckoo said, "Polo, I'm finta go take a shit at my bitch crib, I'll be right back."

"Hurry up, we need that heat out here," Polo told him.

Cuckoo trotted off. Over his shoulder, he said, "I said I was nigga."

They had gotten the line down and a tall male addict was behind two middle-age women that stepped up to the porch. When it was the tall guy's turn, he paid Polo with some crumpled one dollar bills and stepped into the hallway with Roe. Polo signaled to Roe to give the tall guy one, and then turned his attention back to the next customer. Roe reached his hand in the bag and pulled out a handful of bags, extending his open hand to the customer.

The tall addict checked out the ten or so bags in Roe's hand, but he didn't pick one. He looked around nervously and asked, "Aye, little homie, why don't you be a playa and let yo' boy check out a few more. I ain't trying to be no pest, but that was my last ten. I needs me a boulder."

Roe rolled his eyes, but he obliged by dipping his hand into the bag and pulling out some more crack bags. "Awight now, Slim. Yo' giant ass better pick one, because this is it."

In one smooth motion, the tall guy snatched most of the crack bags from Roe's hand and shoved him backward onto the steps. He darted out of the hallway and Roe jumped to his feet and rushed to the doorway.

"Grab that tall mark!" he shouted. "Get that nigga runnin', he snatched some cracks! Catch his bitch ass!"

The tall crackhead used his long legs to flee across the backyard, as Roe's crew sprang into action. Polo sent a female customer flying as he jumped down off the porch and sprinted after the thief. L.J., Big Tee and a bunch of other teenage gangsters joined the chase. The man led them out of that courtyard and through several more before he was about to run past a boy standing on the edge of a row house.

L.J. shouted ahead, "Aye, Family, stop that nigga, he bogus! Get his ass!"

The boy acted like he wasn't going to do anything, until the man was almost past him, and then he neatly gave him a foot sweep. The crackhead did a front flip and tumbled after being tripped. Before he could get to his feet, the boys chasing him pounced on him. They punched, stomped and kicked him quickly into submission.

"Look out y'all!" Big Tee commanded as he slowly jogged onto the scene of the thrashing. In one of his hands, he carried a blue milk crate.

Some of the boys were slow to move at first, but quickly got out of the way as the fat teenager started beating the fallen crackhead with the crate. The victim balled up on the ground and screamed for mercy as Big Tee rained blow after blow on his head, shoulders and back. Soon though, Big Tee ran out of gas and had to lean against the wall; the other boys resumed beating the tall man. L.J. looked around and noticed that a small crowd had started to form. He started pushing the young boys back.

"That's enough, that's enough," L.J. ordered.

"Hold on, y'all grab his right arm and unfold it." Polo said.

They rolled the man over and one of the boys unfolded the crackhead's arm. Polo stomped his hand open and picked up the crack bags he had stolen. He put them in his pocket and tossed one bag back onto the injured man's chest.

"That's the one you paid for bitch," Polo said before walking away.

"Awww, hell nall," Big Tee said. He walked over and

scooped the bag off of the crackhead's chest. "His bitch ass made me run. He ain't gettin' shit."

"Bring y'all ass on, ain't nobody back there securing Roe," L.J. ordered.

They pushed their way through the small crowd and headed back to their courtyard to continue their business. The crowd quickly grew disinterested and dispersed.

....

Back in their courtyard, they resumed business as usual. Polo returned to his post and Roe had never stopped serving during all the commotion. L.J., Big Tee and a few other boys in their clique were standing around recounting their roles in the excitement, when Cuckoo walked up to them.

Big Tee spoke first. He said, "You missed it dog! Where the fuck you was?"

"I told y'all I was going to take a shit. What happened?"

"Soon as you left, a bogus ass clucker snatched some rocks and tried to run," L.J. said. "We hawked his ass down and stomped his ears together."

"Stop playin'," Cuckoo said in disbelief. "That ain't never happen. Y'all bullshittin'."

"Nigga, we ain't playin'," Big Tee said. "Yo' shitty booty ass missed it. Homie was in line when you left. That tall ass nigga with them Chuck Taylors on. We beat the brakes off his ass, two backs over. He prolly still laying there."

"Which back?" Cuckoo asked with piqued interest.

"In the back that Frito got killed in last year," a squeaky voiced teen named Percy offered. "In the back behind Candy Lady Theresa row house."

"Yeah, I know that back," Cuckoo said. He fell silent as he listened to their accounts for a few moments. They were all laughing at Big Tee being out of breath after the chase, when Cuckoo said, "I almost forgot y'all, I gotta run to the crib and check on my little sister. I'm comin' back."

....

In the courtyard behind Theresa the Candy Lady's row house, the tall crackhead pulled himself into a sitting position with his back against the wall. He moaned with any little movement because his entire body ached. He was bleeding from his head, his left eye was swollen shut and his mouth was busted. Using the hand Polo stomped, he dug into his pocket, wincing from the pain the entire time. The cigarette he fished out of his pocket was broken beyond repair so he tossed it away.

He chuckled, but it hurt so much, he had to stop and hold his chest. He spat blood from his mouth and clutched his ribs. He leaned his head back against the wall and closed his eyes. Though his eyes were closed, he felt someone standing over him. He opened his eyes to see Cuckoo Carl standing there with an evil grin on his face pointing a gun at him.

"Damn, I done really bullshitted myself," the tall man observed.

"Yup," Cuckoo Carl agreed.

"I guess I can cancel Christmas, hunh?"

"Pretty much."

"Don't suppose you in the mood to give a nigga a break?" the crackhead asked.

"Nope."

They both looked into one another's eyes for a moment, before the injured addict dropped his eyes. At first, the man looked scared, and then he seemed to suck it up. He looked up at Cuckoo again with his one good eye.

Defiantly, he said, "Well, fuck it then little nigga get on with it! I ain't finta suck yo' dick or nothin'..."

Cuckoo obliged him by pumping all 17 shots from his nine millimeter into the tall man's chest, stomach and legs. The man slumped over on his side as he slipped into his death throes. Cuckoo squatted down on his haunches and watched every moment of his victim's demise. When the crackhead stopped kicking and moving about, Cuckoo stood up.

He looked around the backyard until he found a brick. He began to disassemble the pistol, putting the pieces in his pocket. The last piece of the gun that contained the barrel, he used the brick to smash it beyond repair. Without ever looking back at the tall man's body, he left the rear courtyard and walked back to the courtyard where his crew was located. Along the way, he wiped off the individual pieces of the gun and dropped them into several different sewers.

CHAPTER TWO

Cuckoo Carl was lounging on the couch in the living room of Cindy Brady's row house with his gun on his lap. He was watching Big Tee and Roe play a videogame on the television with semi-interest. In the corner of the room that doubled as the dining room, L.J. and Polo were sitting at a table bagging up a freshly cooked quarter key of crack in dime bags. It was a heated battle on the Super Nintendo game console, but eventually Big Tee lost the game against Roe. The chubby youth tossed the joystick on the couch.

"Man, fuck that game, I wanna watch that Girl Gone Wild tape," Big Tee said.

Roe laughed. "Yo' soft ass just mad because I was beatin' that ass. You can't fuck with me and I keep tellin' you that. Mortal Kombat is my shit, fat ass boy."

"All you do is that bitch ass Get Over Here shit," Big Tee lamented.

"Nigga, I know you ain't talking. All yo' ass do is that bitch ass foot sweep," Roe countered. "Either that or keep freezin' a mufucka."

"Man, fuck all that," L.J. interrupted. "Turn to Jerry Springer. This bitch I know finta be on there today, I think."

Roe switched the game console off and picked up the television remote. He changed the channel looking for the popular talk show, but a local news program caught his attention. The news reporters were all gathered in a Chicago Police Department press conference. The police superintendent was standing at a podium next to a table loaded with wrapped kilos of cocaine.

"Aye y'all, check this shit out." Roe said. "Polo, L.J. look at this y'all. Look at all that fuckin' yay on the table. Damn that's a lot of coke!"

The boys all crowded around the television.

"Damn, look at all them books!" Polo exclaimed. "They just fucked somebody up."

"Shit! Shit! Shit! Shit!" L.J. repeated, with a look of pure disgust on his face. "Ain't this 'bout a bitch!"

Roe asked, "What, G? You actin' like that's our work. That ain't our coke."

L.J. rolled his eyes at Roe as he sat on the arm of the couch. "Everybody, shut the fuck up, I'm trying to hear! Roe turn that shit up."

The police superintendent said, "...in a routine traffic stop. The driver appeared to be disoriented and drove down a one way street in the wrong direction. The Columbian nationals driving the truck displayed suspicious behavior leading to a search of the vehicle, where a ton of cocaine was discovered and seized. Questions?"

"Motherfuck me that was a lot of coke!" Big Tee said. "What if we had all that fuckin' yay?"

"Hell fuckin' yeah," Cuckoo agreed. "If we had all them bricks, they wouldn't be able to do shit with us. We would lock down the whole fuckin' city. I would be the mothafuckin' mayor."

L.J. wasn't participating in their little game of fantasy. He slid off the couch arm onto the couch next to Cuckoo with a sickly look on his face.

"Fuck is wrong with you, L.J.?" Roe asked. "Look y'all, L.J. just seen all them keys get bumped and he done got sick."

They all laughed, except L.J.

"You niggas is dumb as hell," L.J. snapped. "The same thing make you laugh will make you cry."

L.J.'s ominous, unexplained warning set off another round of laughter.

"What the fuck is you even talkin' about?" Polo asked. "You act like that was our coke that got bumped. You tweakin' fam, you better stop smokin' all them blunts. What is you trippin' about, we got yams!"

L.J. sat forward on the couch. "I'm not tweakin'. You little slow mothafuckas is the ones tweakin'. Y'all slow asses don't even realize what just happened. All that coke on that table was coming here. That's Chicago's supply for probably the next six months. Just watch, the streets 'bout to be fucked up. Watch what I tell you."

Disgusted, L.J. pushed himself up and off the couch. He returned to his seat at the table and began again packaging the crack for street sales. Without looking up from his task, he said, "Y'all ass better pay attention and get ready for this shit. That wasn't the throwaway load, the coupla books they let get bumped so they can get the big load through. Don't be no fool, that was the big load. It's gone be a minute before the cartel put together a load like that to come this way. If you know like I know, save every penny you can because it's about to be fucked up. It's finta be a drought."

"Man, Charlie, don't say no shit like that," Polo said. "You really think it's gone be a drought?"

"I know it is. Remember, I told you niggas. Damn! Shit was going too fuckin' good, it never fails. This some bullshit. I need me a drink. I'm 'bout to get drunk as hell. One of y'all get Cindy Brady so she can go to the store."

Roe jumped up from his seat and walked over to the closet in the corner of the living room. When he opened the door his aunt Cindy was sitting in a chair wearing a blond wig, braided into two pigtails. She tried to close the closet door back, but Roe held it open.

"Monroe, don't start playin' with me, you little black mothafucka," Cindy Brady warned. "I ain't for none. Close the fuckin' door and leave me alone. I don't wanna hear y'all fuckin' mouths talkin' 'bout Cindy Brady done stole shit. So, I'm just gone stay in my closet until y'all ass is done."

"Auntie, that's yo' tweakin' ass. Ain't nobody said you stole nothin'. If we did, we wouldn't be fuckin' with you. Chill out, Cindy Brady, L.J. want you to go to the store."

Cindy Brady stood up. "Y'all ain't gotta say it. I makes sure it ain't no way you can say it. So when y'all bagging up, I takes my blast and come sit in my closet so won't nobody never be able to say I took shit. Ain't finta be no excuse for crazy ass Carl to shoot me. That sick bastard just be itchin' to shoot somebody. I bet even you and Tee, my own nephews and my own first cousin Leon, would let him do it, too. Y'all ain't shit! That's why I'll be right here in my closet. I bet you won't get Cindy Brady. Now get out my way, Money."

"Yo' wig on too tight, Cindy Brady," L.J. commented. "Ain't nobody tryin' to shoot you. Now, come on out that closet ole crazy girl and go to the store for me, cousin. I want me a pint of Bacardi. Anybody else want somethin'?"

Polo pulled a wad of money from his pocket and peeled off twenty dollars. He dropped it on the table. "Get me two of them apple Boone's Farms and a book of Tops."

"I want like five dollars' worth of hot meat with some crackers and a Sprite," Cuckoo Carl added.

"Get me a grape Crush and eight different 25 cent bags of chips so I can make me a mix," Big Tee said.

"Anything else, your majesties?" Cindy Brady asked as she walked around the room and collected their money. Roe followed her to the apartment door. Cindy Brady looked out of the peephole first and then opened the door and peeked out. She slid out of the narrow opening and Roe locked the door behind her. He went over to the table and began to help L.J. and Polo by counting the crack bags they had packaged already into 50 bundles.

"L.J.," Roe said, as he tied a knot on a bundle of dime bags.

"Waddup, Family?"

"You really think it's 'bout to be a drought, nigga?"

L.J. thought about it for a moment. He said, "Yeah, it's almost for certain with the amount of shit that just got bumped. It fuck around and be one of the worst we've ever seen, too. That was just too much coke. It'll be quite a while before they put another load together of that size and send it this way. I guarantee you, they just hurt the Chi and the Midwest with that one. Like I said, save yo' money."

CHAPTER THREE

Cindy Brady stood over the Pyrex pot on the stovetop in the small kitchen of her row house apartment. It was so hot in the kitchen the brick walls were sweating; but that didn't stop Roe, L.J., Cuckoo, Big Tee and Polo from crowding in the small space with her. Furiously, Cindy Brady stirred the pot with a well-used butter knife, dropping a few cubes of ice into the potion every few moments.

"What do you think, Cindy Brady?" Polo asked anxiously.

Irritated, she answered, "I can't fuckin' tell yet. I'm trying to slow cook it with the ice because it ain't rockin' up. I'm trying to get all the bullshit off of it. It shoulda been started to rock up, but it won't get tight. I'm about to take it off and see what it do. Gimme some more ice."

She took the pot off of the stove eye and held it over the sink. Big Tee took a bag of ice from the fridge and put it in the sink. Cindy dumped a few handfuls into the water and continued to whip the oily water as they all stared at the pot. As the substance cooled down, it began to form into a grayish mass.

"I think we got something here," Cindy Brady announced.

She removed the chunk of product from the water in the glass pot and placed it on a mirror on the kitchen counter. L.J. took a razor blade and sliced off a piece of crack. He slid it in front of his cousin, Cindy Brady.

"Check it out and let us know what's to it," L.J. said.

Cindy Brady produced her pipe and lighter as if by magic. She started going through the ritual of placing her steel wool pad and turning her lighter up, when she looked up into their faces.

"Oh, hell nall, y'all. Get the fuck up out my kitchen. Y'all ain't finta be sittin' in a bitch face while she take a swang. Get y'all ass outta here. Give me a minute and I'm gone let y'all know what's up."

The crew trooped out of the kitchen and went into the living room. They draped themselves over the couch and chairs and made small talk while they waited for the verdict. Roe and Big Tee turned on the Sega Genesis to play Sonic, while Polo, Cuckoo and L.J. started up a domino game. Moments later, Cindy Brady walked into the living room. Immediately, they all stopped what they were doing and looked at her eagerly. Sadly, Cindy Brady shook her head.

"Nothin'?" Polo asked

"Nothin'," she replied.

"Nothin', nothin'?" Big Tee asked.

"The shit ain't nothin'. It gave me a little freeze and that's it. That big piece I just smoked, I should be high as hell, tweakin' right now."

Everybody looked disappointed, but Polo looked angry. He pulled his cell phone from the holster and dialed a number. He stepped outside on the front porch to place his call. Soon he could be heard arguing with someone on his phone.

L.J. banged his fists on the table. "Fuck! I knew it was too good to be true. A eighth a key in this drought and for only five gees?"

"That's fucked up, Family!" Big Tee spouted. "We was finta come up, too. I was finta bag up some micro-dots. Straight match heads. It's so dry out here, we coulda got that shit off with no problem. I was already countin' that bread."

Polo came back inside the apartment and banged the door closed behind himself.

"What happened, Family?" Roe asked.

Polo was seething as he said, "Man, this bitch ass nigga, Ice, that sold us that bullshit, tryna say the shit was good when he gave it to me. He said that he know about us project niggas and we always be tryna do some slick shit. He said that he gave us straight butter, not no comeback, so we can gone with that bullshit."

Cuckoo asked, "It sound like the nigga not tryna kick back

our bread, is that what I'm hearin'?"

Polo sagged into a seat at the table. He took a cigarette from the box of Newport shorts on the table and lit one. He reported, "That nigga said he ain't kickin' back no ends. Said we gotta get it like Tyson got his title."

In response to what Polo said, Cuckoo Carl laughed wildly.

"Ain't shit funny, nigga," Big Tee said disgustedly. "His hoe ass got our fuckin' money and he talkin' foxy on the phone. How the fuck is that funny?"

"What's funny is that nigga wanna get his family together for a few thousand dollars," Cuckoo replied. "Funerals cost way more than five gees."

"Yeah, but that's besides the point," Roe said. "It's rolling out there. Crackheads is everywhere and ain't nobody got shit. What the fuck we gone do 'bout some work? We ain't got no work or our cash."

L.J. said, "You niggas actin' like y'all new to the game. We can't even worry about that nigga right now. He let us know how he feel. We'll catch up to him later. Right now though, we got a gang of this garbage ass coke and that shit gotta get sold. We finta bag up like 900 dimes. That'll be enough to get our money back with a few extra dollars for everybody pocket. Anybody come back complainin' too hard, we kick em back they bread. Lot of they ass ain't got high in a coupla days so we should be able to get rid of this shit with no problem. What y'all think?"

Everyone was in agreement.

"Hold on, hold on," Cindy Brady interjected. "I want me a cut, and not crack. I want some cash. Before y'all get to talkin' shit, just give me $50 now and a ride to 47th Street real quick. When I come back and put this whammy on this bullshit, nothing but the true old school smokers will know it wasn't real, and you can bag up another 200 bags, easy."

Polo didn't say a word, instead he went into his pocket and tossed three 20 dollar bills on the table. "Pay somebody to take you up there."

Cindy Brady put the money in her bra and left the apartment.

CHAPTER FOUR

The Family members, consisting of Roe, L.J., Cuckoo, Big Tee and Polo, along with ten or more of their crew were sitting on the cars in the parking lot in the rear courtyard. They weren't hustling though, there were no drugs to be had. They were smoking weed and drinking forty ounces of beer.

Big Tee uncapped a 40 of Olde English and took a long sip.

"Damn, greedy ass nigga, pour some out for the niggas that ain't here," Polo said.

"Fuck them, they shoulda been they ass here," Big Tee countered. He was about to take another drink, but he caught the disapproving look on L.J.'s face. He poured out some beer first, and then took a long drink.

"This really is some bullshit, G," Polo said while shaking his head. "It's been almost six weeks since we were workin'. I can't last much longer, I'm 'bout to pawn my jewelry."

"That's what jewelry for, nigga," Cuckoo commented. "If you fucked up, that shit gotta go, Family. Shid, I'm 'bout to sell my Park Avenue to Taco from 59th. I'm just gone have to ride my Regal."

"My stupid ass had the nerve to be gamblin' at Swayze's the other night," Polo said. "Lucky, I didn't lose nothin', though. They had me stretched out for a minute for like $1200. You shoulda seen me, I was sweatin' like a nigga on trial for murder, with a bitch that hate me as my only witness. I got back with a coupla ten to fours and I folded my tents. I went to the bar and bumped into my old man."

"Yo' pops a real nigga," L.J. said. "What he was on?"

"He wasn't on shit. I told him this drought had us fucked up and he said he can get us whatever we need. I think he was frontin' for this thick ass Mexican bitch he was with. He say he got some crystal white for sale. I think he bullshittin' though."

Roe said, "I hope he wasn't because we need that shit. This drought shit fuckin' up everything. I wanted to buy me a box Chevy for my birthday, but the way this shit lookin', I'm gone be buyin' a bus pass."

They all laughed, but Big Tee got up and stood over Polo. He said, "Fuck all that, Polo. Was yo' pops serious?"

"I don't know, I mean the nigga used to be heavy back in the days before he went to the feds. He look like he was doin' good. He had a bankroll on him and he was cleaner than a Northside sissy. He told me to come holla at him at his car lot on Western."

"What the fuck is wrong with you?" L.J. asked. "You just now mentionin' this shit, and you ain't went to holler at him to at least see if he tellin' the truth or not? We over here starvin' and yo' pops is tellin' you he got food, and you won't even go check to see if the shit is real?"

"Whateva, nigga," Polo answered. "I wadn't even thinkin' about that shit. I was happy I won my fuckin' money back. After that, I started gettin' drunk with Camisha and went to her crib, fucked her and passed out. I forgot all about that shit. It really just came to my mind while we was sittin' here talkin'."

Cuckoo's cell phone rang. Before he answered it he said, "Camisha freaky ass made yo' geek ass forget about ev'rything." Cuckoo opened his phone to answer it as he stepped away from the group. After a short conversation, he returned to the group with a huge smile on his face. He was excited as he blurted, "I know where that nigga Ice is right now. One of my wolves just peeped him at the Mickey Ds politickin' with a bitch. I been needin' some action, too. I'll be right back, Joe."

Cuckoo trotted to his car and Polo jumped up to go with him.

"I'm goin', too," he announced. "We bought that bullshit on my word. That was my deal and I got us fucked. I'm on this one with you, Cuckoo."

L.J. grabbed Polo's arm. "Nall, nigga. Let that man go huntin'. That's what he do. We need you to take Roe and Tee to go see what's up with yo' pops."

Polo removed L.J.'s hand from his arm. "Later for that shit, I want in on this nigga Ice. That nigga think he did somethin' slick with his bitch ass. Ain't nobody takin' nothin' from the Family and getting away with it. On top of that, his hoe ass had the nerve to talk shit on the phone."

"Man, calm yo' ass down, Joe," L.J. ordered. "You heard what the fuck I said. Let Cuckoo go handle that business. You go get up with yo' pops and see if that shit he talkin' is real. This is just as important as that, maybe even more so."

Cuckoo Carl hopped into his Regal and fishtailed out of the parking lot. He straightened up the car and zoomed away, making a right turn at the corner. For a few moments, Polo stared after his car, looking like he wanted to protest, but he knew it was a waste of time.

He pulled his car keys from his pocket and motioned to Roe and Big Tee. "C'mon you two and don't be arguin' and shit, neither. And keep y'all dickbeaters off my radio."

CHAPTER FIVE

At the McDonald's restaurant on King Drive, Cuckoo Carl slowly drove through the parking lot. He was trying to catch a glimpse of his prey Ice, while taking care not to draw attention to himself. On the north side of the building where the drive-thru window was located, he spotted Ice talking to a girl by his cream colored short body Cadillac. Cuckoo averted his eyes as he rode past them and exited the parking lot. He reentered the lot from the South side, drove to the rear of it, and parked his car.

He took out his gun and ejected the clip to check its capacity. He reinserted the clip and jacked a round into the chamber. He pulled a pair of leather driving gloves onto his hands before opening his car door as quietly as possible. Quickly he checked his surroundings to make sure no one was paying attention to him, and that there weren't any cop cars in the vicinity. Everything looked normal, so he pulled his gun out and crept up on the unsuspecting pair.

Before Ice and the woman could react, Cuckoo was upon them. The woman started to scream, but he slapped her and put his finger to his lips, warning her to be quiet. Instantly, tears welled up in her eyes and she stood there holding her jaw. Cuckoo turned his gun on Ice.

"Get them fuckin' hands up, Ice Ice baby," Cuckoo snarled. "Waddup now, nigga?"

Ice did his best to remain cool. "Ain't shit up, nigga. I don't know you, homie. I ain't got no beef with you."

"Nall, you don't know me, but you know my business partner. You sold him some bullshit and then told him to get his money back the way Tyson got his title. Sound familiar? Yeah, you remember. Big mistake, bitch ass nigga. You coulda kicked our little bread back and I wouldn't be standing here now."

Ice rolled his eyes to the sky, and then stole a glance into his car. Alerted, Cuckoo followed his gaze and spotted Ice's gun on the passenger seat.

"Now that was stupid," Cuckoo remarked. "Much shit as you talk, you shoulda had yo' gun on you, 'specially when you know you be sellin' people bullshit drugs in these Chi-town streets. I suppose you thinkin' about tryna to get to yo' gun, hunh? Don't be stupid, you gone make it to the morgue way before you make it to that pistol. Now slide out the way and let me get over there. Slowly nigga, before I put a hole in yo' stomach."

Cautiously the two men traded places and Cuckoo took the gun off the seat without ever taking his eyes off of Ice. He stuck the gun in his rear waistband and as he did, he noticed a book bag on the seat.

"What's in that bag?" Cuckoo asked curiously.

"Nothin'," Ice replied with a slight shake of his head.

"For some strange reason, I don't believe you, bitch." Cuckoo pointed his gun at the shocked woman. "Baby girl, can I trust you to reach in there and open that bag for me, and not do nothing to make me have to shoot you in the head?"

The woman nodded her head as she reached into the car, picked up the bag and unzipped it. Cuckoo smiled when he saw the bag was full of money.

"Wow, Ice! That's a whole lotta nothin', nigga. Looks like our five gees with a little extra thrown in for interest, and for wastin' our fuckin' time. Plus, I'm gone need a little bit more because of your terrible customer service."

"Look man, that ain't my paper and it belongs to some people that don't play," Ice warned. "You don't wanna touch that, boy."

Cuckoo poked Ice in the head with his gun. "Nigga, what made you think I play about my fuckin' money. You's a dumb nigga anyway because you worried about they money when you should be worryin' about yo' own ass."

Ice realized this situation had way more potential to go

south than he'd previously assessed, so he tried to explain. He said. "Look man, I wasn't sayin' it like that. My bad, I thought the shit was good and that maybe y'all had played with it. Why don't you take the five gees, I owe y'all, plus another gee for your troubles and we good then. My fault..."

"Yeah, yo' fault, yo' mistake," Cuckoo said right before he shot Ice several times in the chest and once in the head when he fell. He looked at the woman. She was looking like a deer caught in the headlights of an 18-wheeler.

"Did you see who did this to him?" Cuckoo asked.

"I didn't see nothing," the woman said, her voice shaking with fear.

"Hand me my bag," he said. "Remember now, you didn't see anything. If you tell somebody you did, I'm gone find you and give you exactly what he got. You feel me? Now turn around and close your eyes."

Shakily, the woman handed him the bag, closed her eyes and then turned away from Cuckoo. "Please don't kill me. I didn't see anything, please, please."

Cuckoo came close enough to press himself against her butt as he whispered in her ear. "Remember how easily I found this hoe ass nigga. Don't make me have to find you, too."

"I'm not, I swear I didn't see a thing. Please don't kill me. I don't know nothing. If you let me live I won't say anything."

Her pleas went unheard because Cuckoo had shouldered the bag, tucked his gun away and slipped back to his car.

CHAPTER SIX

Paul "Frenchie" French Sr. sat at the desk in the trailer that served as the office on his used car lot. Polo, Big Tee and Roe crowded into the room and stood in front of his desk. His girlfriend, Martina sat on the corner of his desk with her painted-on skirt hiked up on her big legs. She snorted a fat line of cocaine off of a small mirror.

Frenchie said, "Martina, baby, you remember my son Paul Jr. from the other night at the gambling spot?"

"Polo," Polo corrected.

"My bad, Polo and that's his friend Terrell, I mean Fat Tee."

Roe and Polo laughed, but Big Tee rolled his eyes. "Nall, Frenchie. It's Big Tee, man."

"My bad, my bad," Frenchie apologized as he took the mirror from Martina. "You is fat, though. Who is this little nigga? I don't know him."

"Everybody call me Roe or Money."

Frenchie looked Roe up and down, before snorting two lines of coke. He handed the mirror back to Martina and wiped his nose. "Nigga kinda young ain't he? He real?"

"As can be," Roe stated.

"Papi, your manners are terrible," Martina said. "Boys, take a seat, please. Would you like a beer or any other refreshments?"

She held out the mirror to the boys.

Big Tee said, "I'm good on the yay, but I'll take a beer and some of them Ruffles on that fridge."

"I'm straight," Roe said.

They all took seats and Polo accepted the mirror from her. He inhaled a couple of lines and handed the mirror back to Martina. She placed it on the desk and walked over to the refrigerator, and got Big Tee and herself a beer. She took one of the large bags of chips from the top of the fridge and handed it to Big Tee, along with his beer.

Frenchie looked at them. "Alright, lil niggas, I know this ain't no social call. So, what's up? What you tryna buy? I got plenty of inventory, some shortbody Caddies, a coupla Park Avenues and a new 'Vette. We can go take a look and I can get you into something nice as long as you got some cash."

"Nall, we ain't looking for no car right now," Polo told him.

"Well, what can I do for y'all? Spit it out, I ain't about to try and read y'alls' mind. Don't worry, you can talk in front of her, she good."

Polo looked at Martina for a moment, and then back to his father. Martina offered him the mirror again and he took it. He did another line and handed the mirror back. He tried to clear his throat several times and shook his head as if he was trying to clear it.

"Damn that's some good C," Polo commented, as he reached his hand up to touch his face. "Man, my whole fuckin face is frozen. That's the shit we need right there. Can you get us some of that there?"

Frenchie's interest was aroused. "Just how much are we talking? Just so you know, I don't really deal. It's got to be worth my while to cop some yayo for anything more than recreational purposes."

Roe waited for Polo to speak, but he seemed to be having some difficulties making his mouth work right. He saw that Big Tee was preoccupied with stuffing his face with Cheddar and Sour Cream Ruffles, so Roe knew it was up to him.

Roe threw caution to the winds. He said, "We ain't been able to get ahold of shit for almost three months now. This drought is crazy, got niggas goin' broke. Ain't shit out there but straight bullshit. Niggas is sellin' drywall and comeback. The last shit we had was straight B12 and it still went like hotcakes. This drought done damn near put us out of business."

Frenchie leaned back in his swivel office chair. "I ain't know it was bad like that. I knew it had been slow for a minute, though. This drought shit is bad for all of our economy."

"Frenchie, do you got some more of that shit there?" Roe asked anxiously.

"Yeah lil' nigga, that's what my people got. That's straight off the boat. The product is there, but you still ain't said what you little niggas is tryin' to do. I know you niggas over there in them bad ass projects could use a nice piece."

Roe looked at Polo, but he was still out to lunch. He looked at Big Tee and the heavyset teenager shrugged his shoulders. Somehow Roe remembered his big cousin L.J. teaching him to never make the first offer.

"You know what, Frenchie, I don't even know what we can afford. This drought got us so fucked up! All I can really say is, let me know the cost of the shit and I'll let you know how much we can afford."

"Ok," Frenchie conceded. "Well, right now, all I gots my hand on is a half a pie. It's from my personal stash, and I want 25 for it. I'm not piecing it out, neither. Either y'all buy the whole thing or nothing. No fronts either, you hand me 25 gees and I hand you yo' shit."

Big Tee choked on the sip of beer he was taking. "Hold on, Frenchie, that's crazy as hell, man. 25 gees for half a bird? Damn man, at least pull out yo' gun if you gone rob us."

"Terrell, I know you a fool, but I hope you ain't a damn fool. Think about it, slow ass boy, that shit is pure than a mothafucka. That's flake, boy! Y'all can play with that shit and turn them 18 into 36 and y'all will still have the best and only product in them damn projects. I'm actually giving y'all a deal because y'all my son people."

Roe looked over at Polo. His friend was numb, he couldn't speak, all he could do was swallow and sniffle. Polo's state made the decision for Roe. "Frenchie, we finta get that money together. Don't sell that, we want it."

"Okay, lil' nigga," Frenchie agreed. "I'm giving y'all asses 48 hours and that's on the strength of my son, but don't take too long. Remember you study long, you study wrong."

"We comin' back to get that," Roe promised. "Come on Tee, help me get this nigga to the car with his high ass."

....

Big Tee and Roe helped Polo into Cindy Brady's row house,

and deposited him on the couch. L.J. and Cuckoo were sitting at the table, playing Dominoes and drinking Crown Royal. They looked up as they saw their friends dump Polo onto the sofa.

"Fuck is wrong with him?" Cuckoo questioned.

Big Tee made a cocaine snorting motion. "Nigga got happy with the booger sugar."

"Diz-zamn," L.J. said. "That's all he had? He look fucked up."

Roe flopped down on the couch beside Polo. "That's it. The nigga went numb, couldn't even talk. I guess he been snortin' so much weak ass coke, when he got hold of some real shit his system shut down."

"We got good news and bad news," Big Tee announced as he accepted the blunt Cuckoo offered him. He took a long pull off of the blunt and had to pause because of a choking fit. When he spoke again, he had tears in his red eyes. His voice was strained as he said, "The good news is Frenchie do got some coke. He said he got a half a pie of the shit that got dumb ass right here fucked up."

"That's good news nigga, what's the bad news?" L.J. asked.

Big Tee wheezed, "The nigga want 25 gees for the mothafucka. He ain't tryna to piece it out, and he said no fuckin' fronts."

Excitedly, L.J. and Cuckoo exchanged the Family handshake with one another.

"We bout to take over this whole fuckin' project!" Cuckoo exclaimed. "Hell fuckin' yeah!"

Roe was dumbfounded. He said, "Maybe you niggas ain't hear us. We said that nigga want 25 gees for that shit. We ain't got no 25 bucks right now. I don't see what the fuck y'all so happy about. We gone have to sell everything we got in the next two days, just to get that shit. And that's if he still got it."

Without answering, Cuckoo left his seat at the table and picked up a backpack on the floor by his chair. He walked over to the flimsy coffee table in front of the couch where Roe and Polo were seated. He unzipped the bag and dumped stacks of cash onto the table. Roe sat forward and picked up a bundle of bills.

"How the fuck you get this?" he asked.

Cuckoo winked at him. "Let's just say it's a personal loan from Polo's boy, Ice. It's more than 25 there, we gone have some change left over." Cuckoo placed 25 thousand dollars back into the bag, zipped it up and tossed it onto Polo's lap.

L.J. stood up and brushed off his clothes, he turned his snakeskin hat from the back of his head to the front. "Go get that asap from Frenchie," he said. "Look in that fridge and see if there's some milk. If there ain't none, have Cindy Brady go get him some so he can bring his ass down. I'm outty 5000, finta go get me some pussy."

L.J. picked up his keys from the table and left out. Roe locked the door behind him and took his seat again.

"Ain't no milk in there," Big Tee told them.

"Nigga, how you know that?" Cuckoo asked.

"I wanted some cereal earlier and I looked in there and wadn't no milk."

"You fat as hell," Roe stated as if he'd just realized that for the first time.

"Fuck you, Roe, little ass pack of noodle eatin' nigga. I'm not fat, I'm big boned."

"Yeah, yo' bones big as hell too, you fat fuck," Cuckoo joked. "You must got buffo-potamus bones."

"The fuck is a buffo-potamus?" Roe asked with a laugh.

"The son of a buffalo and a hippopotamus like his fat ass," Cuckoo replied.

"Man, fuck y'all," Big Tee said. "Where Cindy Brady at? She ain't in the closet again?"

"Nall, she upstairs with her little boyfriend," Cuckoo said. "That lil' drunk ass nigga that always be gettin' beat up."

Roe walked over to the bottom of the flight of stairs that led to the second floor. He yelled, "Auntie! Auntie! Check it out, we need a store run!"

They heard Cindy Brady's bedroom door open and then she clip-clopped down the stairs. She stood on the last step and looked at them. "I'm telling you ghetto bastards now, y'all buyin' me a beer, and a wine for my man. And you cheap mothafuckas is buyin' a family pack of pork chops so I can smother them bitches with some onions and rice. Now, what y'all want from the store? And what the fuck is wrong with Polo ass, why he lookin' like that?"

CHAPTER SEVEN

The back courtyard where the Family's crack dealership was located was doing turn away business. At times, the lines were wrapped around the building. Once they got the half a key from Frenchie, they cooked it up with Cindy Brady's help and tripled their investment. They all sat down at the table and bagged up the smallest rocks they could. They rode around the projects and passed out a few samples to get the word out, and by the time they made it back to their courtyard to open up shop, there was a stampede of customers.

They were ready for the rush though, thanks to L.J.'s careful planning. Cuckoo Carl and his small army of juvenile delinquents made the crackheads get into orderly lines; while Big Tee and his junior hustlers, led by Squeak, ran bundles and collected the money for them. L.J. took Polo's spot on the porch, and Polo joined Roe in the hallway to collect the buyers' money while Roe handed them their purchases.

As a customer came out of the hallway with his purchase, L.J. said, "Next five, hurry up and shut the fuck up. Have yo' money ready."

The next five customers stepped up onto the porch and entered the hallway one at a time. They each paid Polo and then stepped over to Roe. The third customer in that batch, handed Polo a rumpled 10 dollar bill and walked over to Roe. Roe reached in the grocery bag and handed him a bag of crack. The customer didn't walk away, instead he held the small baggie up to the light.

"Hell nall! What is this shit?" the customer complained. "I don't want this. This ain't even a fuckin' matchhead! I wouldn't even pay a nickel for this lil' shit. Man, lil' nigga, let me pick a better one for my money. How you just gone give me somethin'? Let me pick my own shit! Fuck you think this is?"

Roe started to get mad at first, but instead he smiled as he said, "You know what dog? You right. Gimme that one back and move to the side."

The customer handed Roe the bag back and stepped to the side with a smug look on his face.

"Aye, Polo give this tough Tony ass nigga his money back and send the next customer," Roe said.

The customer realized a moment too late what was happening. As he watched the next few customers get their crack and leave, some of the air left his chest.

"Lo, give this nigga who think he gone tell us how to run our business back his money, so he can get the fuck out the hallway. He said he gotta pick his crack and since we don't do that, he should take his business elsewhere."

"Fuck him Roe, I ain't givin' his ass shit back. He paid for one and if he don't want that one, then that's on him. Now, he better get the fuck on before he be leavin' this bitch with a limp."

With a menacing look on his face, Polo pulled his shirt up displaying the handle of his pistol. Realizing he had really bullshitted himself, the crackhead swallowed hard as beads of sweat popped up on his forehead.

Humbly, the guy apologized. He said, "My fault y'all. I don't know what the fuck I was thinkin'. Just give me a bag and I'll get out y'all way, no hard feelings."

"You gone be the nigga with the hard feelins, big mouth," Roe commented, as he continued to serve the customers that entered the hallway.

"Please little homie, please, that was my last lil' money. Please don't do this, just give me a bag and I'm gone."

Roe asked, "Pole, what you think Family?"

"I don't give no fuck, Roe. Fuck him either way, but whatever you gone do, do it now because he need to get his ass out this hallway."

"You know what my man? You lucky I'm in a good mood, so I'm gone do something for you." Roe dug down deep into the shopping bag of crack bags and purposely chose the smallest bag he could find; he handed it over to the crackhead. "There you go nigga, next time you won't complain. You gone take what the fuck you get and get the fuck on. Now do yourself a favor and let all yo' crackhead buddies know, ain't no pickin'."

Clutching his super small bag of crack, the disappointed man turned to leave the hallway. Watching the crestfallen man walk away made Roe laugh as he continued to serve customers. On the way out, Polo kicked him in the ass. The man was so broken, he didn't even say anything just walked away holding his butt.

Moments later, Big Tee stuck his head in the hallway. "What happened to homie that walked outta here holding his ass cheeks?" he asked.

"He just had to learn to put a eye on his lip and watch his mouth," Polo said.

Big Tee laughed. "Polo, you need to call Frenchie and see can we get some more of this shit because we halfway done when y'all finish that. And we need to... Damn! Yo' ass smell like you dead!"

He was referring to an exceptionally smelly, dirty customer that walked into the hallway. In such a small space, her body odor was oppressing. Her hair was a matted dirty mess and her clothes were tattered, greasy and filthy.

The woman said, "Fuck you, you dick eatin', booty lickin', fat, funky pussy lovin', spoiled titty milk drinkin', lard ass piece of donkey shit. Now, give me one and that shit better be good."

The lady dug into her grimy panties and pulled out a slimy looking $10, which she attempted to hand to Polo. With a look on his face like he was holding back vomit, he wouldn't accept the bill from her.

"My money good, you dickless, fuckin' worm," she snapped as she waved her sawbuck around. "Ain't you niggas sposed to be gangstas? How you 'fraid of a lil' pussy sweat? Bitch ass, baby teeth havin', goat ass fuckin', cum drinkin', aborted baby fetus fuckin', son of hoghead cheese eatin' bitch! I want one of them cracks and I got money!"

"Just drop it on the floor," Polo instructed. "Give her one Roe, so she can get the fuck outta here!"

The lady licked the bill and placed it gently at Polo's feet.

Roe hurried up and gave her a bag of crack and she left the hallway. As the woman walked past Big Tee, she jumped at him and he jumped backwards. That made her laugh wildly as she retreated from the courtyard. Polo kicked her money to the side before walking out of the hallway, followed by Roe.

To the waiting crowd, he announced, "We on hold for five minutes! Don't start talkin' shit or you won't get served when we open back up." To L.J., he said, "We gotta let that mothafucka air out. That bitch stank!"

"Call Frenchie while you ain't doin' nothin'," Big Tee suggested. "That bitch was funky than a mothafucka, I ain't never smelt no shit like that."

Polo used his cell phone to call his father. "Pops, waddup my nigga. I need you like never before."

"What you need, lil' nigga?" Frenchie asked as he fingered the two kilos of coke on his desk.

"Please tell me you got some more C and that it's that same shit. We needs a lil' bit more, too. They lovin' that shit down here. We almost through with what we got."

"Didn't I tell you that Frenchie got you? I got some of that same shit for y'all. What you mean by a lil' bit more though?"

"We need a whole thang this time, Frenchie," Polo said. "Can you handle that?"

"Nall, young buck, the question is can y'all handle that? The ticket on them is 50 gees, but since you family, I'll go 45? You got that?"

"That's all?" Polo joked. "Nall, I'm just talkin' shit Frenchie. We do need that asap, though."

"Alright, well I'm gone be right here waitin' on y'all. And bring that lil' nigga Roe with you. Tell him I got two Chevy Broughams out here now. He keep talkin' about he want one, tell him I said put his money where his mouth is. Don't take too long neither, I'll sell this mafucka."

Polo hung up the phone and looked at all the crackheads gathered in the yard. He turned to Roe. He said, "C'mon nigga, we back in the hole. We should be able to finish the rest of these real quick, then we gotta make a run."

"Shop back open!" L.J. yelled much to the crackheads' delight.

....

Down the street from Frenchie's car lot, in the back of a tortilla delivery van, two federal agents sat listening to the conversation between Frenchie and Polo on their wiretap on his office phone. When their conversation concluded, the two agents looked at one another and then exchanged a high five.

The first agent said, "Looks like you were right, Jim. I owe you a corned beef sandwich from Manny's Deli."

Jim said, "Doug, I told you this piece of shit Frenchie was dirty. I knew he couldn't go straight. I just felt it. I'll make a call and alert the drug boys, let them know what's going on. This'll be like shooting fish in a barrel for them as sloppy as ole Frenchie is, and whoever this Polo fella is."

Doug got up from his seat at the listening post and walked to the driver's seat of the van. "Let's go get that corned beef," he said as he started the van. "Our friend Frenchie isn't going anywhere."

CHAPTER EIGHT

Roe drove onto the main street that cut through the middle of the projects. Row house apartments, walk-up apartment buildings, low-rise buildings and several huge buildings lined the streets of the square mile housing development. As Roe cruised the blocks of the jet where he'd lived all of his 16 years in his North Carolina blue Chevy Caprice Brougham, the loud music coming from the trunk could be heard for a block in either direction. The chrome and gold Cragar 30 spoke rims and fresh Vogues tires on the big sedan gleamed in the afternoon sun.

He was wearing a fresh, Denver Broncos Starter jacket and a matching snakeskin Broncos hat cocked to the side. A pair of white, blue and orange Bo Jackson Nikes with the matching sweatshirt and a crispy pair of creased Girbaud jeans completed his outfit. Around his neck and coming to rest on his chest lay a huge gold herringbone with a large anchor charm. The fresh hairdo his female passenger was sporting bobbed up and down in his lap as she gave him head as he drove. He had to remember to keep a cool look on his 16-year-old face though he wanted to break into a huge grin.

Leaning extra hard as he cruised, Roe honked his horn and nodded his head at different people as he rode by them. Triumphantly, he drove onto the block where the Family's open air drug market and Cindy Brady's row house was located. There, he pulled as close to the curb as he dared to with rims on his car, and put the Chevy in park. Polo, Big Tee, and Cuckoo along with several Family soldiers were sitting on Polo's BMW watching their young homie in disbelief.

Felicia, his passenger, sat up and adjusted her new Bulls Starter jacket and small gold herringbone necklace with a charm that read FEFE resting on her neck, while Roe adjusted himself and zipped his pants. She pulled down the passenger side sun visor and looked into the mirror. She applied a fresh coat of lip gloss before closing the sun visor again, and inserted a stick of Juicy Fruit gum into her mouth.

Roe got out of his car and walked around to the passenger side where he opened the door for Fefe. She was older than him by several years. She got out of the car and gave Roe a passionate kiss on his neck. He cuffed both of her butt cheeks and squeezed them tightly. When they broke their embrace, she grinned at the Family members watching them. Roe took several Breyer's shopping bags off of the back seat and handed them to her. She licked his neck again and switched away as Roe watched transfixed.

"Damn, lil' cousin you ain't playin' no games," Big Tee said. "How the fuck did you get her? And what you gone do with all that, lil' nigga?"

Roe laughed as he took the champagne bottle Polo was drinking from him and took a gulp. He made a face as he looked at the label. "Why the fuck is you drinking this shit? Champagne is nasty."

Polo took his bottle back. "I wouldn't expect a busta' like you to understand. And ain't nobody ask you to drink it no way. Champagne and cocaine is for players, young ass street punk. Stick to smoking that stinky ass skunk weed and drinking 40s and Golden Champale."

Big Tee rolled his eyes. "Yeah, alright Scarface, wipe your nose. Fuck all that though, Money Mothafuckin' Roe, how in the hell did you get up with Fefe thick, pretty ass? And do Rhonda, little rowdy ass know?"

Roe rubbed his head as he leaned against Polo's car. He took a Philly blunt from his pocket and used his finger nail to split it. He extracted a coin bag of weed from his jacket pocket, and did his best to remove the sticks and seeds before dumping the contents of the bag into the belly of the blunt.

Without looking up from the blunt he was rolling, Roe said, "Man, Rhonda ass pregnant. I gave her stupid ass some money to get a abortion, and this bitch gone go buy baby shit with the cash. We got into it about that shit! Here it is, I'm expectin' her to be at the crib not feelin' good and shit, so I go check on her. She at the crib dancin' around in her room, organizin' all the baby shit she done bought. She get to talkin' 'bout help her put the baby bed together. I went crazy on her ass. She wasn't tryna to hear shit though, talkin' 'bout she keepin' it. I'm tryna tell her I ain't tryna be nobody fuckin' parent."

"Aye, Roe, you know if you need me to...," Cuckoo started, making a gun with his two fingers. The look Roe gave him stopped that idea in its tracks. "My bad shorty, I was just trying to help."

"I see you got scratches on yo' neck and face," Big Tee observed. "How that happen, nigga?"

Roe licked his blunt to seal it. "I was just gettin' to that. So, I'm tryin' to tell her that she need to go to the chop shop and this bitch talkin' 'bout baby names. Before I knew it we was going at it in her momma crib. I was fighting her sisters and her momma. Shit was crazy! She broke my fuckin' Eric B And Rakim rope chain! If she wasn't pregnant, I woulda stomped her ass."

Cuckoo said, "Quit sellin' those wolf tickets, nigga. Rhonda and them whupped yo' ass up there. Shid, she been whuppin' yo' ass since 5th grade when she first made you go with her."

"You ain't lyin'. She been beatin' yo' ass, Roe," Polo agreed. "We used to have to get her up off you back in grammar school."

"Fuck y'all, I like it rough," Roe joked.

As they were laughing at Roe, a new sports coupe with dark tinted windows drove onto their street. The obviously expensive automobile cruised slowly in their direction. Cuckoo noticed the car before anyone else. He lifted his shirt and put his hand on the handle of the pistol resting in the waistband of his pants.

"Heads up y'all, anybody know this car?" Cuckoo asked.

They all looked at the vehicle in question. Polo said, "Nall, I ain't never seen that car before. Not around here, I would remember a whip that look like that."

Polo reached under the seat of his car and retrieved a gun from under it. He made ready as the car came abreast of them. The car's windows were raised, but they could still hear music from the car and the driver was playing the Geto Boys, My Mind Playin' Tricks On Me. The driver's door opened slowly causing Cuckoo Carl and Polo to raise their weapons.

From inside the vehicle, L.J. shouted, "You scary ass nigggas bet not shoot my mothafuckin' car, I know that!"

Their friend got out of the car and both teens lowered their guns. The battle-ready look on their faces were replaced with grins as they greeted him.

Cuckoo Carl put the safety on his gun before he tucked it away. He shook L.J.'s hand with the Family handshake and walked around the car. "Boy, you almost got this pretty bitch shot up. Me and Polo was about to put some bullet holes in this slick lookin' mothafucka. We ain't know who the fuck you was behind them dark ass tints."

Big Tee and Roe walked over to the car and looked at it more closely.

"Man Joe, what the fuck is this, L.J.?" Big Tee said, as he poured Cheetos in his mouth from the large bag he was eating. "This boy raw as hell."

"It's a Lexus coupe and watch it Charlie, yo' fat ass spittin' food," L.J. warned.

They all walked into the street and examined the car. A small crowd began to gather to view the vehicle, also. Roe sat in the driver's seat and held the steering wheel as Big Tee squeezed in on the passenger side and turned up the radio. As they were examining the car, a Chicago Housing Authority police department car rolled up behind them and hit the lights. L.J. motioned to Roe to pull the car out of the middle of the street and into a parking space. He parked the car and got out, so did Big Tee. He used the key remote to arm the alarm and lock the doors. They walked over to their friends, as the CHA officers put their car in park and got out of it. They approached the boys.

"Aye, you. Is that your car? Let me see your license." one officer asked Roe.

"Why? I ain't drivin'," Roe answered.

"You were just driving," the other office stated.

"He was parkin', not drivin'," Polo said. "That ain't the same."

"You ain't gotta show no CHA cops no license," L.J. said

with a snarl. "Y'all ain't traffic cops."

"We weren't talking to any of you boys, we're talking specifically to him," the second officer specified getting in Roe's face. "This ain't none of y'all fuckin' business."

"Get out my face man, fuck is wrong with you!" Roe snapped.

"Shut up, boy!" the officer shouted and slapped Roe's snakeskin hat off of his head.

The expensive hat flew off of his head, sailed several feet and landed upside down in a pile of dust. Without so much as a word, Roe swung and hit the CHA officer in the jaw. The other officer rushed toward Roe, but L.J. scooped him by the legs and slammed him on the ground. The other Family members jumped in, some helping Roe fight the bigger, older and heavier officer, and the others stomping and kicking the officer L.J. had body slammed.

A long 15-passenger van with CHAPD decals on the side screeched to a halt and five officers jumped out to join the fray. One officer tried to hit Big Tee with a nightstick, but he jumped back. Before the officer could recover, Big Tee surged forward and punched him, knocking him out cold. Another officer grabbed Roe in a chokehold and Cuckoo pulled him off of Roe. The officer spun around and swung at the same time, succeeding in catching Cuckoo with a right hand. Cuckoo fell on the ground and Polo punched that officer out. Cuckoo recovered and got to his feet. He pulled his gun and stood over the officer, aiming his gun at the unconscious officer's head. L.J. noticed him about to execute the CHA policeman, and rushed over and grabbed Cuckoo's gun.

A short, Black woman officer noticed L.J. standing over her downed comrade with a gun in his hand and pulled her gun. "Drop that gun!" she yelled.

Though L.J. dropped the pistol, the female officer triggered off two rounds, knocking him off his feet. Everyone stopped fighting as if someone pushed a pause button. The other officers drew their weapons at the sounds of the gunfire, and one of them shot in the air. L.J. was on the ground writhing in pain.

"Everybody get the fuck on the ground now!" shouted the officer that fired into the air. All of the fighters complied, except Cuckoo Carl. Instead of lying on the ground, he bolted. Two officers gave chase, and the other officers immediately began cuffing the guys lying on the ground. They were helped by another van full of CHA officers arriving on the scene.

By the time the officers that chased Cuckoo Carl came back empty-handed, the scene was pure chaos. There were paddy wagons being filled with Family members, an ambulance leaving the scene with L.J. and plenty of the project's residents had shown up and they didn't particularly like what they were witnessing.

The more and more people that joined the crowd, the more of them learned that a CHA cop had just shot L.J. As the ambulance was driving away someone threw a beer bottle, and then someone threw a brick at one of the paddy wagons. A small chunk of concrete smashed an officer in the face making him drop to his knees. His comrades came forward to help and more garbage and bricks rained down on them. While the project cops were preoccupied with the rock throwers, a slim woman with a finger-wave hairdo casually walked over by the police vehicles. Skillfully, she used an icepick to flatten the tires of one of their vans, and two of their cars. Someone threw a five gallon can of white paint onto one of the cars and it also spattered on the officers. A red, chitterling pail full of old cooking grease was thrown onto another car.

The crowd was becoming more and more hostile by the moment, so the officers decided to retreat. Nearing their vehicles for the first time, they noticed their now handicapped autos. The crowd behind them pushed forward as their attacks grew increasingly aggressive. One of the CHAPD white shirts wearing sergeants fell next as someone threw an ironing board that smacked him in the face. His fellow officers picked him up, and they all piled into the vehicles that were still operable and zoomed away. The crowd cheered as they left, but as the cheers died down, everyone just stood around.

Polo walked over to his car and got his gun. He walked over to the CHAPD van and shot it until his clip was empty. Several more men stepped out of the crowd and shot the cars too. The crowd roared and attacked the vehicles. Someone lit the car on fire covered in grease and soon thick black smoke billowed into the air.

....

Big Tee, Polo and Roe along with five of their Family members sat in a holding cell at the CHAPD area precinct. They were talking amongst themselves about the afternoon's events when a turnkey officer came to the cell and unlocked the door. He swung the door open.

With a bored look on his face, the turnkey said, "Paul French Jr., Terrell Princeton and Monroe Pearson, front and center. Let's go." As they stepped out of the cell into the corridor, the turnkey instructed them, "Nose and toes on the wall, hands behind your back." One by one he handcuffed each of them. "Now follow me single file."

"Where we goin', turnkey?" Polo asked.

"Yeah, where you takin' us?" Big Tee added. "Fuck is y'all on?"

"Oh, and I forgot, shut the fuck up!" the turnkey growled.

The journey wasn't long, they went out of the holding cell area, through two heavy steel doors, and up a short flight of stone steps. On the next level the turnkey officer opened a room door and directed them inside. The boys stepped inside the room; it contained only a table with two chairs and a steel bench against the wall; there was a two-way mirror too.

"What the fuck is this?" Polo asked.

In a monotone voice, the turnkey said, "Shut the fuck up and have a seat on the bench."

When they were seated, the turnkey unlocked the cuffs from behind each one of their backs, leaving one on their wrists, and the other he locked to a steel pole on the wall. When everyone was secured, he turned and left.

Roe asked, "Man, what the fuck is goin' on?"

"I don't know, but whatever it is, it's some bullshit though," Big Tee answered. "I'm surprised they ain't separated us. Whatever the fuck is goin' on, when they come in here, we don't know shit."

"Shut the fuck up fat ass nigga, they listenin' to us now," Polo told him.

They all fell silent and shortly the door to the room swung open. A large, Black detective walked into the room. On the table he placed a gun, their property bags, and a plastic evidence bag full of drugs. He took a seat at the table across

39

from them and surveyed them for a bit, rolling his toothpick around in his mouth.

"Lookie here, lil' niggas, my name is Detective Seals. That gun there got two bodies on it from your project. There's enough heroin in that bag to get you all 9 to 45 with ease."

'That shit ain't ours," Polo protested. "Man, they bought us in here for fightin', not no heater or no drugs. We ain't got shit to do with that."

Detective Seal said, "That's not how this shit is getting wrote up. If I say the gun and drugs are yours, they are until you can prove otherwise."

"Man, Joe, we don't know what the fuck you talkin' about," Big Tee said.

"If you would shut the fuck up, I could tell you what I'm talking about," the detective declared. "Those niggas is down there tearing shit up because of y'all and the nigga that got shot. Leon Jones is stable. He gonna make it. So, I need you lil' bitches to stop that damn riot."

"How we gone do that?" Roe asked.

Detective Seals rolled his eyes. "Lil' nigga, I was just getting to that. You are going to get your black asses on the phone and call whoever you need to call, to tell them to chill the fuck out. If not, you niggas are going to jail."

"Again, we in here, how the hell is we sposed to do that?" Polo asked.

"Y'all better get to calling people and telling them to stop," Det. Seals said. He pushed their property bags over to them. Polo and Big Tee took their cell phones from the bags, they dialed as Roe made suggestions of who to call or beep. It took a couple of minutes, but their phones began to ring as their Family members started to return their calls. Hurriedly they explained to their fellow project dwellers just how important it was for them to chill out. Several high ranking gang members from their housing development assured them they would squash it.

To the detective, Big Tee said, "They chillin' now. Niggas is gettin' they guys under control. You ain't gone still put that shit on us is you?"

Detective Seals collected their cell phones and put them back into their property bags. He stood up and put the gun in his holster.

"That's yo' gun?" Roe asked.

"Yup. If there's any consolation there are two bodies from your neighborhood on it for real."

"I guess that ain't real heroin neither?" Polo asked.

"Coffee creamer," answered Detective Seals.

"Ain't that bout a bitch!" Big Tee said. "We just went for the okey-doke."

"Pretty much," Detective Seals agreed as he prepared to leave the room. "But don't be too mad, I done made fools outta niggas way smarter than you street punks. Alright fellas, y'all will be out of here in a coupla hours, they only charging y'all with trespassing."

Detective Seals had his hand on the doorknob to leave, when Roe asked, "So was you lyin' about our guy, too? He ain't dead is he?"

"I wouldn't lie about something like that. Like I said, he's gonna make it. He's stable. You niggas will be out in a few and you can give him my regards. Tell him Detective Seals said, catch you later."

When the detective left the room, they talked amongst themselves until the turnkey came to return them to their holding cell.

CHAPTER NINE

Cuckoo Carl, Roe, Big Tee and Polo got off the elevator on the floor of L.J.'s hospital room. They were all dressed in dope leather jackets, jogging suits or blue jean suits. Their gold chains and gold rings were huge and extremely noticeable as well as their new gym shoes. They reeked of weed and alcohol and fried chicken because of the several huge bags of Popeye's chicken they were carrying. They weren't using their inside voices either as they walked through the hall, causing them to be on the receiving end of several withering stares from staff and patients. A young, pretty CNA grinned at Roe as he walked in front of their group, leading them to L.J.'s room. Roe smiled back and made a mental note to double back on her after their visit with his older cousin.

At L.J.'s room door, Roe knocked twice on the door before entering. L.J. was sitting on the side of his bed in a hospital gown looking at his lunch tray with complete and utter disgust. He turned at Roe's knock.

"Waddup, Family," Big Tee said as he placed a bag of chicken and side dishes on L.J.'s tray table. "We had to come through for you. I knew you was tired of eating this slop. This shit one step above County jail food."

"My mothafuckin' niggas," L.J. said with a huge grin. He reached out to shake hands with Big Tee, who did so heartily, crushing him in an embrace. His affectionate hug turned L.J.'s grin into a grimace of pain.

"Let go of his hand, you big, clumsy animal!" Cuckoo snapped, pushing Big Tee. "The fuck is wrong with you, the man just got shot and yo' big goofy ass all on him. Get the fuck on."

Undaunted, Big Tee stood there. "Fuck you Polo, I'm happy to see my cousin. My bad L.J. Shid, when that bitch ass CHA cop shot you, we thought yo' ass was done. They was salty because we was beatin' they ass."

Everyone else crowded into the room and shook L.J.'s hand, too.

"I'm happy to see you niggas too, but what's up with some of this bird?" L.J. queried.

Big Tee dug into the bags and began laying out a spread on the tray table and the nightstand. The crew shucked their jackets and began to tear into the feast.

As they were eating, Polo asked, "L.J., why you up a banger on them CHA's anyway?"

"I didn't, that wasn't my gun," he replied. "Aye, hand me them red beans and rice."

"That was my heater," Cuckoo confessed. "I was about to knock one of them CHA's brains out his head and L.J. grabbed it from me. That goofy ass bitch seen him holding it and her scary ass shot him. He had already dropped the gun. Yo' ass shouldn't have never grabbed my gun, nigga."

Through a mouthful of rice and beans, L.J. said, "You sound stupid as hell. Yo' ass was finta kill a cop because he put you on yo' ass. I don't care if it was a CHA cop. If you think it's hot now, knock one of them mothafuckas off and you gone really see some heat."

"That makes sense," Cuckoo Carl agreed. "But while you been layin' on yo' ass, I done followed that CHA bitch home twice already. They 'bout to be missing a officer real soon."

None of them batted an eye because they knew Cuckoo was serious; dead serious.

"What happened to the gun?" Roe asked. He was eating mashed potatoes and gravy out of one of the large side order containers.

L.J. hunched his shoulders as he ate. "Shid, I don't know, I dropped it right before she blasted my ass. There were so many people out there, somebody must have picked it up. I know the cops ain't got it because I ain't handcuffed to the bed. They actually had a CHA lawyer come up here and try to get me to sign something sayin' it wasn't their fault. They tryna say it was an accidental discharge of the officer's weapon."

"You ain't sign that shit did you?" Polo asked.

L.J. looked at Polo like he'd lost his mind. "What the fuck do I look like to you? I might ain't graduate from high school, but I ain't stupid mufucka. I told him I ain't signin' shit. I got two words for they ass: law-yer."

Big Tee stopped ripping through the spicy chicken breast he was currently dismantling as a thoughtful look crossed his face. He looked up and said, "Aye, Family, lawyer is one word, I think."

Roe, L.J., and Cuckoo all laughed at Big Tee.

Polo said, "Will you shut the fuck up, Tee, you sound slow as hell. It's fucked up when people think you slow, but it's even worse when you open yo' mouth and remove all doubt, dumb ass."

"Fuck you, Polo," Big Tee said.

L.J. continued, "Then they sent a couple of they bitch ass detectives up here to try and scare me. I rolled over on they ass. I told them come back with me some breakfast, some sausage, pancakes, hash browns and scrambled eggs with some orange juice. They ass was mad, too. I told they ass beat it cause they'll be hearing from my lawyer. I'm suing the shit outta CHA ass and them rookie ass police."

"Where all they get you at?" Cuckoo inquired.

L.J. lifted the cast on his arm. "In my arm obviously, it broke it and in my side. That one went straight through. I was lucky it ain't hit nothin' important."

"That's because yo' ass be eatin' all them gyros and shit," Roe told him. "Keep on... you gone be big as Tee, fat ass."

L.J. laughed, but it quickly turned into a groan. "Fuck all that, what's goin'on with the shop? Is it Family business as usual?"

"Hell yeah, Family, you know this shit don't stop," Polo said.

"Man, all I know is we got to do somethin' about all them damn, funky ass singles," Big Tee complained. "That's some bullshit there, havin' to count them mothafuckas. I be mad as hell! We just had damn near like 3,500 in ones. My fuckin' thumbs damn near fell off counting that shit. The money machine won't take them raggedy muthafuckas."

"We got to stop takin' all them damn singles," Polo stated. "We gave Frenchie like two gees worth of them, his ass called me snappin'. He said he ain't takin' no more than a 100 or two of them from now on. Man, fuck them ones."

"That shit is money, and I ain't lettin' no money get away," Roe promised. "Y'all ass is frontin'. All that shit spends to me."

"Fuck them singles! I'm sick of takin' shorts, too, Family," Big Tee noted. "That shit is gettin' on my nerves. Really, I'm sick of sellin' dimes. We coppin' way too much shit to be bagging up dimes all got damn day. Ain't no drought no more, let's do something else."

L.J. tossed a balled up napkin into the tray of chicken bones in front of him. He swung his legs up into the bed and laid back. "That shit been on my mind too, since I been in here. It's time to step this shit up. First, it's time we start pushin' weight. The drought is over, but we still got the best prices and the best coke. Me and Polo gone be handlin' that when I get out of here."

"What me and Tee gone be doin' then?" Roe asked, as he held out his hands. "Throw me one of them corns."

Cuckoo Carl tossed him a corn on the cob.

"Y'all still gone be baggin' up," L.J. notified them.

"Fuck me!" Big Tee exclaimed.

L.J. laid back on his bed and closed his eyes. He said, "No more dimes, all twenties from now on. If the Family shorties wanna sell dimes, they gotta cop some pieces. We'll get them started though, front them what they buy. And yeah, we ain't takin' no shorts, no change, and no fuckin' singles. We gone give the crackheads one week to get used to it, then we ain't even takin' fives no more. We gone use Cindy Brady's trick and puff that shit up to make the bags big as fuck, too."

The other four teens looked at one another. Looks of approval shone on their faces at L.J.'s plan.

Polo spoke first. "I like the sound of that shit, all twenties. That shit gone cut down on some of that extra traffic, too. If you ain't got $20 then get the fuck on."

"No singles, no fives, no shorts and no change sound like music to my fuckin' ears," Big Tee said.

"This nigga sleep y'all, let's ride," Cuckoo Carl said looking over at L.J.

They all got up and picked up after themselves, throwing their garbage in the wastebaskets. On their way out the room, Big Tee went over to L.J.'s tray table and took one of his two apple pies.

Without opening his eyes, L.J. said, "Put my apple pie back you fat fuck. I'm finta get some sleep, these pain meds kickin' in. This the shit we need to be sellin' in the streets. Polo figure out how to get ahold of this shit and our kids' kids will be rich."

The guys laughed as Big Tee put the apple pie back, but he snagged a chicken leg and some French fries.

Before turning on his uninjured side, L.J. added, "I'm out this bitch tomorrow or the day after, with or without the doctor's say so, y'all. Roe be on point to come pick me up. In something besides that hot ass Chevy."

Roe slipped on his jacket. "Alright Family, but don't forget it was yo' car that started all this shit. Hit me on the hip when you ready though, I'ma scoop you."

They left the room and walked to the elevator. Big Tee danced along with them as he ate his food. He was humming and grinning between bites.

"What the fuck you so happy about, nigga?" Cuckoo asked, as he pushed the down button to summon the elevator.

The elevator doors opened and Big Tee danced onto the car. "You wanna know what I'm so happy about? No shorts, no singles and no fuckin' change."

They all grinned, but just before the elevator doors closed Roe jumped off the car.

"Where you goin'?" Polo asked.

"Don't pull off, I almost forgot, I gotta get this nurse number."

The elevator doors closed.

CHAPTER TEN

In a large briefing room at the Federal Bureau of Investigation building, agents from several different agencies were convened for an early morning briefing. The briefing hadn't started yet and there was a hum of conversation in the room. The agents of the FBI, DEA and ATF poured themselves coffee and selected donuts and other pastries before taking their seats. While they sipped their steaming java and ate donuts, they walked around the room and looked at the large pictures of the Family that covered the walls of the room.

Everyone from Frenchie to Roe were captured in the pictures; from Frenchie selling cars on his used car lot, to Roe and several of the shorties racing go-karts through the projects. The families' cars, jewelry and clothes were all shown. There were photos of them on shopping sprees, displaying huge wads of cash, shooting dice with thousands of dollars on the ground, drinking expensive champagne, wearing fur jackets, and flashing gold grills. They had been photographed in the projects, in local restaurants, strip clubs and malls.

The door to the briefing room opened and the senior agent heading up this massive task force entered the room. He walked to the podium, placed a folder on it and opened it. He tapped the microphone several times to alert the agents in the room to take a seat. They did so quickly and quietly.

When they were all seated, the man at the podium said, "Good morning. Some of you already know me, but for those of you that don't, I'm Special Agent-In Charge, Thomas Jenner of the FBI. I'm heading up this multi-agency task force in Operation Family Freeze."

One of the seated agents raised his hand.

Agent Jenner nodded at him. "Yes?"

The agent said, "Special Agent Jenner, we've noticed that everyone is here, except the local boys. We aren't working with the State boys, or CPD on this one?"

"The state and city boys have egg on their faces because we, a federal agency, brought this to their attention," Agent Jenner answered. "With that being said, know that their cooperation is going to be minimal at best. They've already decided to mount their own separate investigation, completely independent of ours."

"That's good because the locals can't keep their fuckin' mouths shut anyway," another agent stated.

Several other agents, plus Agent Jenner agreed, as he continued, "We will be proceeding without them. Initially, the IRS was investigating Paul "Frenchie" French Sr. for fraud, tax evasion and money laundering." Jenner indicated Frenchie's enlarged photo on the wall. "During this investigation it came to their attention that French was distributing cocaine to gang members that use the Martin Luther King Houses housing development as their stronghold. As their supplier, he has contributed to the opening and maintaining of several open air drug markets there, plus we have information that they're looking to expand."

"Frenchie is the father of Paul "Polo" French Jr., age 18, also we have Leon "L.J." Jones, who is the oldest of this faction of the Family Members crew at the age of 20. He is the most seasoned of the crew and obviously the leader. Also there's Terrell "Big Tee" Princeton, and Carlos "Cuckoo Carl" Smith, who's a known killer. Don't let the baby face fool you, this kid will kill you as soon as look at you. Both of these two are 17 years old. We've actually had a run-in with Carl Smith before this investigation, so we most assuredly can't wait to put our jewelry on his wrists. Last but certainly not least is Monroe "Roe" Pearson. He's the baby of the bunch having just made 16 years old. He may be younger than them, but he is just as dangerous."

"They've got a crew of minions, but they're not our main concern. We may just throw them to the local boys, let them get the hand-to-hand sales, we want the Continuing a

48

Criminal Enterprise bust. They've got an intricate network of stash houses, workers and wanna-be's so it may take time to unravel it all and get down to the center of this Tootsie Roll pop. We want surveillance up on their drug markets and all of their communication tapped. It's a go."

Another agent raised her hand. Special Agent Jenner pointed to her.

"Sir, what is the deadline for this operation?"

"Good question," Special Agent Jenner said. "I want to be handing ironclad indictments to the US Attorney inside of six to nine months."

Another agent raised his hand. Special Agent Jenner pointed at him.

"Is there undercover work? And if so, what's the extent? Just how deep?"

Special Agent Jenner said, "Though we would love to have someone inside, it's highly unlikely. These kids trust one another and no one else. Some of them are actually related to one another, that's why we think they're named the Family. With family around, you don't have to trust anyone else. Again, do not let the baby faces fool you, these are gangbangers and drug dealers from a Chicago housing project, they are typically close to impossible to infiltrate. They are worse than the Mafia. No one, and I mean no one, is going to walk up and get accepted by these guys. You will end up dead in a garbage dumpster or in a vacant apartment if you try to. They don't like new faces unless they're buying, and even then you can't hang around and you better not get caught asking questions. Like I said, we stay on their communication, pay phones, beepers and cell phones. Try a few buys with video surveillance and go from there. If there aren't any more questions, get to work."

CHAPTER ELEVEN

Roe, Polo and Cuckoo Carl stood in the hallway of the fieldhouse that led to the gym. Though it was a little after 10 p.m. there was a Midnight League Tournament basketball game being played on the gym floor. As they chilled in the hallway, with their new clothes and jewelry on display, they were greeted by people going to the game as they entered the building. Fefe walked into the fieldhouse with two of her friends and made a beeline over to Roe and his guys. She hugged Roe, leaving her arms wrapped around his waist.

"Waddup my nigga Polo, Cuckoo," she said.

Cuckoo only nodded his head, but Polo said, "FeFe, waddup with it, Family?"

"Just came up here to see my boo, Roe. I got to keep all these hatin' ass bitches out his face. When these hoodrats don't see you around, they try to trick off with yo' man, but this be me right here. I don't mind if he look at none of these rat ass bitches, but ain't nothin' happenin'."

"She got yo' weak ass in check," Cuckoo said. "Soft ass pussy-whipped ass nigga."

Roe grinned. "You better gone boy. At least I'm getting some pussy. And Fefe watch yo' mouth, I ain't tryna to take nothin' down. I'm chillin'."

Inside the gym, the crowd roared at play.

"You better stay chillin' or I'm gone fuck you up," Felicia threatened. "My bad though, y'all. These is my girls, Pebbles and She-She. Y'all that's Polo and Cuckoo Carl, pay no attention to the mean mug. Cuckoo, you gotta loosen up some, killer."

"I'm good, FeFe, I'm just chillin', this cess bud got me high than a mafucka," Cuckoo said.

She-She sidled up to Cuckoo. "You got some more of that shit?" she asked. "I could use some good reefer. We just bought some bullshit from the buildings, a big ass bag of bunk."

"Weed ain't no thing, baby girl," he said reaching into his pocket and pulling out a baggie of weed. He picked a couple of buds from the bag and dropped them into She-She's hand. "I smoke blunts if you want one."

"Damn, She-She, I like yo' boo's homies," Pebbles said. "These niggas ain't cheap. Y'all put all that in one blunt? Damn! I been hanging in the wrong project all this time."

She-She and Pebbles slapped each other's hands in agreement.

"I don't know what kind of niggas y'all been fuckin' with, but this a everyday thang for the Family," Polo boasted. "We don't roll with Tops or them baby blunts."

Cuckoo was handing She-She a blunt as Rhonda walked into the fieldhouse. She was noticeably pregnant. Roe and his friends were so engrossed in their conversation, they never noticed her until she was standing next to them. One minute she wasn't there, and the next she was. Roe could tell by the look on her face she wasn't pleased in the slightest by what was going on.

"Don't come up here on that bullshit, Rhonda," Roe said, causing everyone to look at her.

"Ain't nobody on shit," Rhonda said. "Quit tryna make it seem like I'm crazy. I just wanna holla at you. I know you moved on as I can see, I ain't trippin'. I need to talk to you outside, though."

Felicia maintained her grip around Roe's waist. "I don't know what business you think you got with Roe, but whatever it is, you can handle it right here. You ain't gotta go nowhere."

"I'm not talkin' to you, FreeFree, oops, I mean FeFe" Rhonda spat venomously.

"Well, you talkin' to my man, boo-boo, so that mean you talkin' to me."

Rhonda rolled her neck. "Oh, so this yo' girl now? So, this yo' girl, Monroe? Speak up nigga, I can't hear you. Is this yo' mothafuckin' girl?"

"Somethin' like that," Roe said smoothly.

"Yeah, you and who else, the rest of the South Side?" Rhonda asked with a laugh.

"Don't worry about me, Rhonda, it sound like you salty," Felicia said. "Don't get jelly now because you had him and lost him. It ain't his fault, he livin' better so he wanted an upgrade. I mean, why wear K-Swiss when you can rock Air Jordans?"

Rhonda laughed again. "Looks more like he downgraded to some L.A. Gear old, used ass boots to me. But enough about that. So Roe, it's over like that? We got a baby on the way and you just gone be up the first chance you get? What type of shit is that?"

Roe unwrapped Felicia's arms from around him and started toward Rhonda, but Polo restrained him. Angrily, he said, "Nall Polo, let me go. I ain't tryna hear that shit. I ain't want no fuckin' kid and I told yo' ass that! I don't wanna be nobody fuckin' daddy, but yo' dumb ass don't wanna listen. Fuck you! I hate you!"

"You wasn't sayin' you hated me, while you was fuckin' me!" Rhonda yelled. "Yo' ass done changed since you got money, now you think you can buy everything and everybody. Fuck you, nigga! How the fuck you gone throw some dirty ass money at me and tell me to kill my child? Nigga, you the one that shoulda been aborted, mark ass nigga! You can let his ass go, Polo. I ain't scared of him and definitely not this skanky ass hoodrat! I'll beat both of they asses!"

Fefe smoothed down her fur vest as she laughed. Before walking away, she said "Roe, you done stressed yo' baby mama out. That cannot be good for the baby. She should thank you though, because the only reason we ain't gone kick her ass for her is because she pregnant. But, really Rhonda, you can save the drama for your mama. C'mon She-She and Pebbles, we ain't come up here for this soap opera shit. Roe, handle yo' baby mama, we'll be in the gym."

"Good riddance, gold digger," Rhonda said as she rolled her eyes. "Just know I ain't gone always be pregnant."

"Why don't yo' ass gone 'head on 'bout yo business, Rhonda? How I even know that's my baby?"

Rhonda's mouth dropped open momentarily. "Nigga, you so fuckin' disrespectful! How the fuck could you fix yo' mouth to even say some shit like that? You ain't got to question where

I been and who I been with, unlike yo' new bust down ass bitch. Ain't no tellin' who dick she got on her breath. Stankin' ass skeezer!"

"Fuck you!" Roe shouted.

"Fuck me? Nall, nigga, fuck you!" Rhonda shouted as she tried to steal on Roe. The only reason she missed was because Cuckoo stepped in between them. He gently pushed her back.

"What you gone do Carl with yo' crazy ass, shoot me? You gone kill me for telling the truth about Roe and his bitch. Y'all letting that money go to y'all head. All y'all. That's ok, because mark my words, Roe yo' ass is gone need me one day. Just watch."

"Fuck I need with a broke bitch with a baby?" Roe asked scornfully. "There's plenty of those around these projects."

Before Cuckoo could react, Rhonda rushed around him and slapped Roe across his face. He raised his hand to return the blow, but Polo grabbed his arm.

"She pregnant, Joe," Polo warned.

"You gone hit me, Roe? Yo' punk ass gone hit me and I'm carrying yo' child?"

"Bitch, I don't care!" Roe seethed. "I woulda knocked yo' block off if this nigga ain't grab me. Get the fuck on you broke, dirty bitch. You just mad 'cause I got money now, bitch, I hate yo' ass."

"You called me a bitch?" Rhonda asked with disbelief. "You called me a bitch? You said I'm mad because you got money? Dumb ass boy, you shoulda stayed in school, I was with you when you ain't have shit, so you should know I don't give no fuck about yo' money. Don't worry about it though, it's all good. I'm gone from it. Move, Carl."

She didn't wait for Cuckoo to move, she pushed past him.

"Rhonda, check it out," Polo called to her.

"Man, let that bitch go, Family," Roe said, as he started to walk away. "Fuck her, we in the gym."

Before Rhonda stormed out of the fieldhouse, she decided to use the bathroom. After using the restroom, she was about to leave, when she walked past the slightly ajar door of an athletic equipment room. She spotted a baseball bat. She suddenly had an idea, so she ducked into the room and took the bat. Instead of using the front entrance, she dipped out of the side entrance of the field house that led to the parking lot.

The parking lot was filled to overflowing with vehicles of all sorts because of all the attendees to the Midnight Basketball League games. Rhonda searched the lot until she found the car she was looking for, Roe's Chevy Brougham. It was parked under one of the parking lot's lights and it had been freshly washed, so it was gleaming in the night. She looked around once or twice, didn't see anyone of consequence so she swung the bat and broke the driver's side mirror. The car's alarm sounded loudly, but that didn't scare her off, as she began to release her frustrations out on the car. With the aluminum bat, she smashed the windows and lights, and banged huge dents into the car's body. People started to take notice, so she ran off into the night, satisfied that Roe and Felicia wouldn't be riding tonight.

As she ran out of the entrance to the park, she never noticed Squeak, Roe's younger girl cousin pointing a pistol at her. "Ooooouuuu! You so lucky you finta be Roe's baby mama!" she fumed, at the fleeing Rhonda. "C'mon y'all," she said to the two boys with her. "We gotta find Roe and let him know that bitch just fucked up his car."

Squeak tucked her pistol back into the back of her black Levi denim jeans and pulled her Pelle-Pelle jacket down. Her long hair was French-braided to the back under her Wing Ding hat with Chitown spelled across the front of it in crystals. The large herringbone chain with a mermaid charm that L.J. had given her for her 14th birthday swung as she jogged around to the front of the building. Inside the field house, they burst into the gym and walked across the gym floor in the middle of the basketball game.

The people in the stands that knew who Squeak and the two boys were affiliated with paid close attention to see what was happening. One of the basketball players that wasn't from their neighborhood, a tall, heavy set guy, looked at Squeak like she was crazy as she walked by. He mean-mugged her and she mean-mugged him back.

"What the fuck is wrong with you shorty, you better get off the floor," the huge basketball player warned.

"Fuck you nigga and this game!" Squeak spat.

"Who the fuck you think you talking to?" the giant rumbled.

54

"I'm talking to yo' big bitch ass," Squeak said matter-of-factly.

The tall guy started toward Squeak, but the point guard on the other team, a local resident, swiftly got between them and put his hand on the big guy's chest.

"Aye, little homie, he ain't know that was you, you know, under that fresh Wing Ding, his bad," the point guard said to Squeak. "It's all good."

Still looking at the big guy, Squeak kept on to the bleachers.

The point guard steered the tall player over to the opposite sidelines, though the big guy was still staring holes in Squeak's back.

"Man, leave that shit alone," the point guard told him. "Them little niggas will leave yo' ass for dead. That little girl ain't no little girl, so get that out yo' head. Plus, it's a nigga over there with them that will kill you right here and now. Just forget about it. Now gone over there to your team."

Over at the bleachers, Squeak greeted Roe, Polo and Cuckoo. To Roe, she said, "Man, cuz, I gotta tell you somethin'."

Roe was seated with Felicia sitting between his legs. "Waddup, baby cuz?" he asked, with a big smile on his face. "What's poppin'?"

"Man, Joe, I don't know how to tell you, but Rhonda just fucked up yo' Chevy, Family."

The smile on Roe's face disappeared as he jumped up, knocking Felicia aside. "What the fuck you say?"

"I said, Rhonda fucked up yo' car, cuz," Squeak repeated. "I wanted to pop her ass, but I know she 'bout to have yo' shorty."

"C'mon y'all," Roe commanded, jumping down from the bleachers.

This time as the group of Family members walked across the court through the basketball game, all of the players minded their business. Roe pushed open a door in the rear of the gym, triggering an alarm. Outside in the parking lot, they all gathered around Roe's wrecked car as he used the remote on his key ring to silence the car alarm. Roe walked around the car several times in disbelief.

"Man, I'm killin' that bitch Rhonda!" Roe exclaimed.

Cuckoo pulled a pistol from his waistband and jacked a

live round into the chamber. He tried to hand it to Roe, but Roe pushed it away. Cuckoo returned the gun to his waistband.

"Gone 'head on, Cuckoo," Roe said. "I'm just sposed to go murk my baby mama? I'm startin' to think yo' ass really is crazy."

"That nigga ain't crazy, he slow," Polo commented as he knelt down next to Roe's car. He rubbed the side of the car. "Well, at least yo' 30s and Vogues is good, and she ain't hit the quarter panels. She fucked yo' shit up though."

"Yeah, she done lost her mothafuckin' mind," Roe said. He had to walk around the car again to notice all the intricacies of Rhonda's handiwork. "Damn, I need doors, fenders, a hood, a trunk, all the windows, the lights. Funky bitch! She bogus as hell!"

A crowd had started to form as the news spread about the damage to Roe's car. Some girls pointed and giggled, and there were people openly smirking in the crowd at Roe's misfortune; Roe noticed them.

"Oh, y'all think this shit is funny," Roe said to them. "We'll see who laughin' when I jump right back down tomorrow. This ain't shit but an excuse for me to cop something new. Y'all tell Rhonda scandalous ass that she ain't done nothin' slick. Oh yeah, and y'all better let her know, that this shit bet not happen again or we gone be to see her, and that's on Family."

"I'm gone go holla at her, Family," Polo said. "You wanna leave it or get it towed?"

With disgust, Roe said, "Don't make no difference, ain't nobody gone touch it. I'm tired of lookin' at it. Let's go back inside and finish watchin' the game."

They were walking off to return to the fieldhouse, but Squeak and her guys stayed behind.

"Roe, you just gone leave the Chevy like this cuz?" Squeak called out to him.

Roe stopped walking and turned around. He took the keys from his pocket and tossed them to Squeak. "That's yo' car now, lil' cuz. Come see me bright and early in the mornin' because yo' lil' ass gone need to make some money to get it fixed."

The smile on Squeak's face was blinding, as she ran and got in her new car.

....

Roe, Polo, Big Tee and Squeak walked up and down the rows of cars on Frenchie's car lot. They had ridden there in Big Tee's Blazer with Tupac's latest CD bumping from the four, 18-inch subwoofers installed in the large kickerbox in the rear of the truck. A tow truck, pulling Roe's Chevy that was now Squeak's car, followed them. When Roe told Frenchie he was coming to buy a car, he told Frenchie about the damaged Chevy and he told him to bring it too. Frenchie also said that he would get it fixed as cheap as possible for Roe.

Since the Family had started buying from him on the regular, Frenchie had purchased more cars of better quality to sell. The prices of cocaine had returned to normal and since he was copping plenty of keys on their behalf, the price he was charging per kilo had dropped drastically. The profits from the coke were nowhere near the same as the drought prices, but it was still pretty good. Frenchie's expansion of the lot's inventory had attracted more customers, too. Many of them found Frenchie's willingness to lose paperwork that should have went directly to the IRS a good reason to shop there.

Roe walked over to Frenchie who was standing by the lot's small garage. He was supervising a porter washing one of the lot's cars.

"Frenchie, ayo, I thought you said you had some good shit out here," Roe said. "Man, yo' ass got Celebrity's and Bonnevilles, I don't want none of that shit."

"That Bonneville SSE is a bad mothafucka," Frenchie commented. "'Especially that white one with that peanut butter leather. Young ass nigga, you don't know quality automobiles. What is you looking for?"

"Somethin' fast. I ain't no old ass man, I want something that ride."

"Well, I showed you a 'Vette, but you said that's a pappy's car. I got one more thing. Nall, nall, nall, I can't sell you that. That's too much car for you."

Roe instantly became interested in whatever car this mystery car was. "Stop it, Frenchie, I can drive. L.J. used to let me drive him around when he was drunk and I was just 12 and 13. What you got? And don't show me no old Smokey and the Bandit looking ass car neither."

Frenchie took a moment to show his porter some spots he was missing on the Iroc Z-28 he was washing. He pointed to the Iroc. "Roe, this one probably is a better fit. This other car got just too much muscle."

"I don't want that shit," Roe said with disgust. "I hate them. Stop playin' and show me the car Frenchie."

"Alright, alright," Frenchie said, acting like he'd been persuaded. "C'mon little nigga. You better have some money too, because you 'bout to get on my fuckin' nerves."

Roe followed Frenchie over to the rear of the lot where several cars were parked and covered. Big Tee, Polo and Squeak walked over to them. Frenchie grabbed a corner of the car cover and pulled it off. There sat a gleaming silver Chevrolet Monte Carlo SS with T-tops and American Racing rims with Goodyear Eagle GT tires. The interior of the car was blood colored with maroon racing stripes and decals on the exterior of the vehicle.

All of their mouths dropped open.

"Dizzamn!" Big Tee yelled. "Gotdamn, that bitch cold than a mothafucka!"

Mesmerized, Roe walked up to the vehicle. Frenchie opened the door and held the keys out to Roe. Awestruck, Roe sat in the driver's seat looking around the vehicle.

"Start it up," Polo prompted him. "We wanna hear this hoe."

Roe turned the key in the ignition and the powerful Chevy growled to life. The engine had a vibrant, powerful sound.

"This is a 1988 Monte Carlo SS," Frenchie said. "A special edition. Ain't no hood niggas ridin' these, but like I said, it's too much car for you. This bitch is runnin' hard, lil' nigga."

Roe held up his hand. "Frenchie stop playin' with me."

Big Tee walked around to the passenger side and squeezed his bulk into the car. He turned on the radio and turned it up. Loud music filled the air. Roe reached over and turned the radio down, all the while glaring at Big Tee. He put both of his hands on the steering wheel. Without looking at Frenchie, he asked, "How much?"

Frenchie took his time as he produced a pack of Doublemint gum from his pocket. He took a piece from the pack, opened it and slid it into his mouth. He looked at Roe.

"You might as well get out of it now and let me put the cover back on," Frenchie said. "This car been completely done, shid, its $25,000 under the hood. All new, high performance shit. The sound system was $10,000 by itself. The interior cost $7,000. This one out yo' price range"

"How much?" Roe repeated.

"Out the door, tax, title and license. Taking into consideration you like family. I'll take 20,000 in cash from you."

Roe patted the gas pedal several times to rev the motor. He cut the ignition and got out of the car. From his jacket and jeans pockets, he produced three rubber-band wrapped knots of money. He held them out to Frenchie.

"This 15 gees, Joe, go get me a temp tag. Put the shit in the same name the Chevy is in."

Frenchie acted like he didn't want to take the money.

Roe insisted, "Man, take it because I'm not giving yo' ass one fuckin' dollar more."

For a moment Frenchie hesitated, but he eventually took the cash. Down the alley, a DEA agent disguised as a telephone worker was high up on a telephone pole with his high-powered camera taking pictures of the transaction.

Frenchie shook his head. "Lil' nigga, you a monster. You sure you only 16? C'mon so I can hurry up and get you out of here, before I lose some more money."

"Hold on Frenchie, what you say about fixin' the Chevy?" Roe asked. "How much you think?"

"My guys will have that looking like new for two gees. One to get started, the other gee when you pick it up, it'll take about a week."

"How only a week with all that damage?" Big Tee asked.

"That ain't shit," Frenchie said. "They got them doors and fenders and shit laying around. That's a real popular car. The hood and trunk, too. They can actually upgrade the front and back lights. The grill still good, and they ain't fuck up the quarter panels."

"Look, Frenchie, let it sit while Squeak run that cash up," Roe said. "I'm gone help her."

"Okay," said Frenchie. "Now come on in the office and do this little paperwork and let me get this temp tag."

"You ain't gotta do that, cuz," Squeak said, as she pulled a bankroll from inside her jacket. She handed two gee stacks to Frenchie. "Tell them gone get started. Cuz, you ain't the only one with a couple of dollars."

"Well, alright then lil' cuz," Roe said with a huge smile. "Once they throw the temp tag on this bitch, you ridin' with me, and we ain't comin' back no time soon. Y'all can gone ride, Big Tee, Polo." Squeak's grin matched Roe's as she waved at Polo and Big Tee before following Roe and Frenchie to the trailer.

CHAPTER TWELVE

On their block in the projects, the Family members were chilling as they watched their daily operation. It had been months since they had to work the packs in the hallway, or run bundles or do security. Their main jobs were copping and chopping the product, cooking and bagging, selling pieces, counting money and finding places to hide the cash and product.

It was lunchtime and they had just ordered pans of chicken and fish for their workers from a nearby JJ Fish restaurant L.J. had invested in. Chicken bones and empty pop cans littered the ground as the workers feasted and tossed their garbage near where they sat or stood. Polo, Big Tee, Roe, L.J., and Cuckoo Carl were sitting around discussing the movie Dead Presidents, when a young gambler named Disco drove onto the block and parked his short body Park Avenue. He got out of the car and walked over to the crew, shaking a pair of dice.

"What they hittin' for? Twenty, I shoot, twenty I hit," Disco said as he rolled the dice out in front of him.

Polo pulled out his bankroll and tossed $40 on the ground. He said, "Shoot yo' shot nigga, and I hope you got some money on you today. I ain't finta be workin' hard to take no c-note from no nigga."

Disco whipped out his knot of money and broke into a dance. He sang, "I'm finta pop that ass, move them thighs, make you niggas butterfly."

They all laughed at Disco's antics as they began the dice game. The lighthearted game soon turned serious as more gamblers joined in and the amounts being betted grew and grew. Onlookers had gathered also to watch and listen to the colorful trash-talking of the gamblers. The dice came around to Roe.

"You niggas done fucked up now," said Roe as he stooped down. "I do this here for my bread and meat, if I don't win then I don't eat. I need a fader not a friend. Back man, get yo' back."

A man named Tony that had just lost the dice ahead of Roe was the back man. "Nigga, you ain't said shit, what you shootin'?" he asked.

"50, I shoot, 50, I hit," Roe replied.

Tony tossed $100 on the ground from his thin bankroll. "Shoot, big money ass nigga. And don't be tryin' that slick ass shot of yours."

"Catch what you don't like," Roe said as he tossed the dice on the ground. He threw a seven, Tony faded him for the $100 again. Roe tossed the dice and rolled them, catching a five as a point. Tony quickly bet him another $100 and Roe promptly rerolled the five taking the rest of the back man's money.

"Somebody else fade this nigga," Tony said in a defeated tone as he rocked back on his haunches. "He too fuckin' lucky for me." He thought, I cannot believe I just lost all my fuckin cop money. What the fuck I'm gone do now? My fuckin' lady gonna kill me!

Someone else faded Roe this time and he threw the dice again, catching a four as his point. The gamblers rushed to bet against him and with him, with Roe covering anyone that wanted to bet him.

"Don't nobody move but me," said Roe as he shook the dice in his hand. "Don't touch it neither if you ain't won it. You niggas think it's sweet because my point is four. Y'all gone be sick when I jump this lil Joe."

As L.J. and the other gamblers were talking shit, Tony looked at all the piles of money on the ground in front of him. A bead of sweat ran down his face, and he gulped as he watched Roe try to hit his point of four. More and more money was added to the bets on the ground. Suddenly, Tony jumped to his feet.

"Blue and whites coming down! Two cars deep!" he yelled.

"Here come the police, y'all!"

As the other participants in the dice game stood up and looked around. Tony grabbed two handfuls of cash from the ground and shot off. Several of them bolted too thinking the police were chasing them.

"Man, ain't no fuckin' cops," Roe said. "That nigga picked up my money. Catch his ass!"

The chase was a short one because Tony tripped over one of the concrete parking lot markers less than half a block away. Before he landed good, Family members swarmed on him, beating, kicking and punching him. They were taking turns stomping Tony, when someone spotted a blue and white CPD cruiser.

"Here come them people for real y'all!" someone called out. "Chill y'all, here come the law!"

They heard the sound of the police car engine as it sped up coming toward them. They stopped beating Tony the thief and tried to walk off, but the police car swerved onto the sidewalk cutting them off. Some of them took off running, and the two policemen in the car jumped out and corralled everyone that didn't run. At gunpoint, the police made them all put their hands on the car while they waited for backup. In moments, several more Chicago Police cars arrived on the scene with their lights flashing and their sirens blaring. One of the first policemen knelt down beside Tony, who was moaning and holding his left eye and ribs.

The officer holding them on the car said, "Tell us who beat this kid up or you're all going for aggravated assault. Whoever speaks first gets a pass. Everyone else is going. This is a one-time only offer so speak up."

Everyone on the car looked totally uninterested in the cop's offer.

"So ain't nobody gone say shit?" the officer asked. "You tough guys would rather go to jail, hunh? L.J., I know you ain't got nothing to say, a kingpin can't snitch."

L.J. ignored the officer's question, but the officer pushed him in the back of the head.

"You heard what I said, L.J."

Calmly L.J. said, "My name ain't L.J., homie."

"L.J., we know who the fuck you are nigger and what you

do," the officer responded. "It's only a matter of time, only a matter of time."

"What the fuck that sposed to mean?" L.J. asked, as he turned and looked the policeman in the eye.

The officer smirked. "Nothing, absolutely nothing. I was just talking shit. So don't nobody know who whupped his ass, hunh? He gonna tell us which one of you gangbanging niggers did it and we gonna lock y'all black asses up. And we gonna upgrade the charges to mob action."

"We ain't touch that nigga, ask him," Roe protested.

"Shut the fuck up!" the cop said as he walked over to Tony as he lay on the ground.

The officer knelt down beside their beating victim and asked him something, but the guys on the car couldn't make out his question. They knew what it meant though when the officer took turns pointing at each of them. Though he was injured, Tony just kept shaking his head though, obviously knowing the rules of the projects: snitching could get you killed. The policeman helped him up off the ground and brought him to the car. "Maybe you can see them better now that you're closer," said the cop.

Tony kept denying that any of them had something to do with his injuries. The officer was noticeably frustrated at Tony's denial. Angrily, he said, "We shouldn't have even called the ambulance for your dumb ass, since you don't know who whupped your ass. We should just leave your dumb ass here and let them finish the job. Don't be scared of these cowards."

Still clutching his ribs, Tony said, "Man, gone with that shit. I ain't never seen these people before in my life. I told you, I was runnin' to the store and I tripped and fell. My ribs is broke though, I think. I should sue CHA for all these raggedy sidewalks."

Both police officers looked at one another. The second officer shrugged. "Cut them loose," he said. To Tony, he said, "Here comes the ambulance."

The other officer said, "L.J., you and the rest of these monkeys can get y'all shit and get the fuck off my car. Get y'all stupid asses in the house or something. If I catch y'all out here again today, before my shift is over, your dumb asses are going to jail for trespassing. Now get the fuck on."

The boys got their possessions off of the hood of the car. They were walking away with scowls on their faces when L.J. turned around to look at the policeman. The officer that had done the most talking pointed his two fingers at him like a gun. L.J. held up his middle finger at the cop and mouthed, "Fuck you," before they headed back into Family Land.

....

Later that evening, Big Tee, Polo, L.J., and Roe were cooling at Cindy Brady's, Cuckoo was nowhere to be found. They had just finished counting the take from the first and second shift. After stacking and separating the money, they rubber banded it into five gee stacks. Big Tee had passed out on the couch and the rest of them were drinking Hennessey and smoking weed, while Polo snorted coke. Roe was busy playing his new videogame on the Playstation while L.J sat at the table, shuffling and reshuffling a deck of cards.

"Aye, Tee, wake you ass up," L.J. said. "Tee! Tee!"

"What man? What the fuck?" Big Tee asked sleepily. "Damn, L.J. what the fuck yo' ass want? Let me get some sleep, my baby had my ass up all night."

"On that noise, Charlie," L.J. said. "I need you woke to hear this shit. Roe, pause that game. Tony Montana, pay attention. How have things been in the Den? Anything weird? Anything look out of place?"

Polo cleared his throat. "Nall, shid, everything been flowin' smooth."

"Roe, pause the fuckin' game, nigga," L.J. said. "Anybody been gettin' locked up?"

Roe put the joystick down. "No man, bullshit like trespassin', maybe a mafucka got caught with a pistol and got a UUW or somethin', but we bonded niggas out. Ain't no Family members snitchin'. Why?"

"I just got a feelin' these weak ass cops know more than they sayin'. That bitch ass blue and white knew my name. We can't start lackin' around this bitch just 'cause we gettin' money. Make sure y'all watch who the fuck be around, too."

"Joe, fuck them polices!" Polo exclaimed. "They ass ain't shit! We done got rich right under they noses. We ain't in them hallways no more. The best thing they can do is catch some of our workers. They ass know all our names, I bet. That ain't

65

nothin' but these Housing Authority bitches tellin' them who we is. Fuck them, the best thing they can do is holler at our lawyers."

"All that's fine and good," L.J. said, as he dealt himself a hand of solitaire. "But you niggas keep y'all fuckin' eyes and ears open there. Make sure y'all on top of any new faces tryna to hang around, too."

"Alright, alright," Big Tee agreed with a yawn. "Is that it, nigga? Can I go back to sleep now?"

"Take yo' fat ass back to sleep, nigga," L.J. said as he placed a three of Spades on top of a four of Hearts. "Just remember what the fuck I said fat fuck, and you two niggas, too."

There was a coded knock at the door, alerting them that it was a Family member. Roe bounced over and looked through the peephole; it was Cuckoo. He let him in and shook hands with him before returning to his game. Cuckoo walked over to the table where L.J. was playing cards and stood over him.

L.J. looked up. "What nigga? Fuck is you standin' over me like the Grim Reaper for?"

Cuckoo threw back his head and laughed. When he was finished laughing, he said, "I'm gone get them to put that on my next custom Wing-Ding. The Grim Reaper, maybe with a skull. Fuck all that, 'member what I told you about that bitch that shot you?"

L.J. looked at him quizzically. "Yeah, what's up though?"

Cuckoo slammed the CHA police officer's badge that shot him down on the table in front of him. "Watch the news tonight, Family," he said ominously. "Don't nobody shoot one of my Family and get away with it. No one!"

CHAPTER THIRTEEN

Roe drove slowly through the housing development with Tupac's Shed So Many Tears blasting from his car's custom sound system. He was headed to the community center for the party that was held there every Friday night during the school year. There was a $2 admission charge that went to the community center.

The SS's trunk rattled from the bassline of Tupac's song as he drove. A tear escaped his eye and rolled down his brown face. It dropped off his chin and landed onto the black fur jacket he was wearing. The matching black Wing-Ding hat on his head was turned backwards. Roe cut across several streets and nosed his Monte Carlo into the parking lot behind the fieldhouse at the park. The entrance was blocked by a garbage dumpster, and when the shorties standing around saw it was Roe, they moved the dumpster out the way so he could drive into the lot.

He pulled into a parking space and put the car in park. Before leaving the vehicle, he checked his face in the sun visor mirror. He was cool, so he got out of the car and walked over to join his Family members. Big Tee handed him a fifth of Hennessy.

"We gettin' fucked up for our nigga 'Pac tonite," Big Tee announced. "I can't believe that nigga dead. It feel like when he died, so did all the love in the world for gangsters, thugs and hustlers. That nigga said the shit we couldn't say."

"Yeah, that shit is fucked up," Roe agreed as he looked around. "Man, we just had to bury Dark Mark, and now Tupac get killed. That shit is crazy. On the Family, I started not to

67

even come up here."

Roe opened up the bottle and poured out some liquor before he took a swig. L.J. walked over to them and Roe handed him the bottle.

"Waddup lil' nigga," L.J. said. "Just warnin' you, certain mufuckas is out here trippin'."

"Who that?" Roe asked.

L.J. indicated Cuckoo, who was walking in circles while he drank from a bottle of liquor and talked to himself.

"The fuck happened to that nigga, L.J.?"

"The law was chasin' Cross-Eyed Kenny and Bravo, and they crashed the stolen car they was in on our block. They hopped out and ran and the law jumped out after they ass. They ran into the back behind Cindy Brady crib and dipped. Long story short, them bitch ass detectives couldn't find them and Razo just so happened to be comin' out of Cindy Brady crib with five bundles of dubs. They thirsty ass grabbed Razo and walked him back up in Cindy Brady crib. They found a pistol in there and put that on her."

As L.J. was explaining Cuckoo's stranger than normal behavior, their disturbed friend walked nearer to them.

"He ain't tellin' you everything, Roe," Cuckoo said animatedly. "Joe, I done been told them bitch ass niggas don't be comin' down our block with them hot ass steamers. Don't bring that shit in Family Land! I mean who the fuck still steal cars anyway just to ride around? I keep tellin' these niggas that y'all bringin' down heat on the guys with that bullshit. I done told they ass more than twice! Now, I'm gone show they ass better than I can tell them as soon as I see they dirty ass."

Big Tee said, "For once I agree with this crazy bastard. Just 'cause they broke ass wanna joyride, we gotta bond Razo and Cindy Brady out. We done lost a pistol and product because of this dumb ass shit. Cindy Brady could even lose her crib under the Zero Tolerance act. You know Housing on that now."

Cuckoo Carl seemed to get even more pissed as he said, "That's costing us even more fuckin' money just 'cause they wanna ride around in steamers. I could even respect it if these niggas was stealin' the mothafuckas and takin' them to the chop shop. Nall, they just wanna ride around the fuckin' projects and make it hot for the rest of us."

"You niggas is gettin' way too fuckin' worked up about this shit." L.J. commented. "This is the fuckin' projects, nigga. Everybody live on top of each other, shit is bound to bleed over into each other's lives from time to time. Shit happens!"

"Shit don't happen to us," Cuckoo returned. "Not us! So you can gone on with that bullshit. L.J., all this money got you niggas actin' soft. Man, Charlie, niggas gotta be dealt with so these niggas around here know that Family Land is off-limits for bullshit of any kind. Them niggas fucked up our money, money they can't pay back neither, so I'm layin' they ass down when I catch them. I put that on the Family! I'm zero tolerance like Chicago Housing."

"Damn, boy you trippin' fam," Roe observed. "If it's already hot from bullshit, you doin' a double murder ain't gone make it cooler, nigga. L.J. holla at this crazy ass nigga."

"You know ain't no talkin' to his ass when he heated like this, so I ain't finta waste my breath. I know yo' ass bet not catch nobody in Family Land over this bullshit. I ain't playin', neither. I hope shorty and nem got enough sense to bounce out south for a minute 'til yo' trigger-happy ass calm down."

Cuckoo was about to reply, but Polo distracted them all. He said, "Oh shit, look y'all! Squeak got that mufucka back right. Look at yo' old Chevy, Roe. She got that hoe clean."

Squeak stopped her car so they could see it. The fully restored sedan gleamed under the street lights. She nosed the car up to the dumpster, but one of the Family members waved her off.

"Ain't no more parkin' spaces in the lot, Squeak," he notified her. "You gotta put it on the street."

Squeak reversed back out onto the street and rode off with Tupac's Ballin' beating from the trunk to look for a parking spot.

"Roe, yo' lil' second in command be doing her thing, hunh?" L.J. asked.

"She our family so you know she got hustler's blood. Squeak doin' good. She can count too, not like these other stupid ass niggas. Her ass be on point and she got her little crew under control. Wish all these niggas hustled like her."

As they were talking, a pre-teen boy walked into the

parking lot and up to them. "L.J., I told the picture man what you said, and he said he ready, y'all can come on now. C'mon, I'm gone take y'all through the side door. They ain't gone let y'all in with them drinks and guns at the front door."

"Thanks lil' man," L.J. said to the shorty. To his guys, he said, "Bring y'all ass on, we finta take a couple of these pictures."

They all looked down at their clothes. Each of them was dressed up, except for Cuckoo Carl. They were wearing slacks, dress shirts, expensive sweaters, leather, suede and fur jackets with gators and dress shoes. Cuckoo was wearing a black Bulls Starter jacket, new Air Jordan shoes, and black Levi's jeans. A gigantic gold herringbone chain with an Uzi charm hung around his neck. A black and red Wing Ding hat sat on his intricately braided hair.

"Damn Cuckoo, we said everybody was sposed to dress up, even the shorties listened," Polo observed.

"I'm wearing my dress gun, nigga," Cuckoo remarked. "Y'all better leave me alone before I don't take shit."

Clutching their bottles of Hennessy, Tanqueray and Moet champagne, the Family members followed the boy into the community center through the side door. Just before the door closed behind them, Squeak and three of her clique slid inside. They walked across the gym floor, through the middle of the party in the direction of the picture man's setup. The partygoers that knew them shook some of their hands, but many of them moved out of the way, letting them pass through with no resistance.

As they walked through, one of the young undercover policemen in the crowd paid close attention to them, though he remained at a safe distance. He walked over near the small kitchen where they were selling hotdogs, potato chips and pops to get a better angle to view them. Quickly, he realized they were only there to take pictures. Just when he assumed they were harmless, Cuckoo pulled up his shirt to display the handle of his pistol in a picture. In that picture, the original Family members had kicked everyone out of the picture except them. L.J. took a seat in the middle of them, with Big Tee and Roe on one side, Polo and Cuckoo took up the other side. The photographer took several pictures like that, and was instructing them to change positions when a teenage gang member walked near the photo set and motioned to Cuckoo.

"That's enough of this shit," Cuckoo announced. He stepped away from the photo backgrounds and over to the side with the boy that summoned him. The boy whispered something to Cuckoo, who in response grabbed him firmly by his shoulder. Cuckoo asked him, "Right now? You sure?"

The boy nodded. "Hell yeah, right now on the benches by the playground. It's some bitches over there, too. I'm sure it's them, Family."

Cuckoo handed the boy the champagne bottle he'd been holding for the pictures and began pushing his way through the crowd.

....

Outside in the park's playground, Cross-Eyed Kenny and Bravo sat on the swings passing a blunt and pint of Seagram's Gin between themselves.

"Man, fuck these niggas," Kenny said as he swung once and stopped. "Them Family niggas act like they own the projects. This is all our shit, I live in this raggedy shit, too."

Bravo gulped some gin. He handed the bottle to Kenny. "We ain't try and wipe out on their block. That shit just happened. Shid, how the fuck we sposed to know we was gone have a blowout? Wadn't shit we could do but bail up out that bitch. What they thought we was sposed to do, sit there in the car and put our hands up? Hell nall! We out this bitch through the backs. It ain't our fault we ghosted them slow ass pigs so nasty they grabbed the first nigga they came across."

"Man, fuck the Family Members," Kenny said, handing the liquor bottle back to Bravo. "Fuck that bullshit, where them bitches go? They had us buy this nasty ass gin and then they ass gone dip."

"I think they rat ass went in the party, Kenny. You know them bitches in there shaking they asses. We would be in there too if them niggas wasn't on that bullshit, got that crazy ass nigga Carl looking for us. Tomorrow we gone go get up with Roe and have him take us to holla at L.J., see if we can squash this shit."

They had been so engrossed in their conversation, they didn't notice Cuckoo's approach until it was too late. Cross-

Eyed Kenny jumped off of the swing to run, but the pistol in Cuckoo's hand stopped him.

"Nigga, I wish you would. Sit yo' dumb ass down!" Cuckoo ordered.

Kenny held his hands up as he sat down on the swing's seat. Bravo took a sip of gin, though his hand was obviously shaking.

"Cuckoo, slow down Family," Kenny said. "We ain't mean for that shit to happen. We'll work that shit off, whatever it is. On everything, we was going to holla at L.J in the morning and get this straightened out. Roe will tell…"

"Man, shut yo' cross-eyed ass up," Cuckoo said. "You talk too fuckin' much."

Without warning, Cuckoo shot Kenny in the head. The slain car thief fell over backward off the swing, but his feet came to rest on the swing seat. Bravo looked on in horror and dropped the pint of gin as he saw his best friend's blood and brains begin to mingle with the wood chips under the swing set.

"What the fuck you gotta say nigga?" Cuckoo asked menacingly. "What, nigga? Say somethin'! I just smoked yo' man in front of you, say somethin'."

Bravo stared at Kenny for a few more moments, and then looked Cuckoo in the eye. He bent over and picked up the gin bottle. He drained the rest of the gin from the bottle and tossed it. He looked back at Cuckoo.

He sneered, "What you think I'm finta beg yo' bitch ass for my life? Nall nigga, I ain't got nothin' to say, do what the fuck you gone do. Fuck you and all them ass-kissin' niggas. I only fuck with Roe and Big Tee anyway. You can suck a dick though, with yo' psycho ass!"

Cuckoo raised his gun to shoot Bravo, just as the undercover cop from the party stepped up behind him, and pointed his gun at Cuckoo's back.

"Chicago Police!" he shouted. "Drop that fuckin' gun now or die!"

Cuckoo hesitated.

"Nigga, I will kill you if you don't drop that fuckin gun right now!" the officer yelled. "Get down on your knees, hands behind your head or I'll fucking kill you!"

Cuckoo tossed the gun into the wood chips as he grinned at Bravo. "They just saved yo' ass bitch ass nigga," he told him as he got down on his knees.

The undercover policeman rushed over to Cuckoo and pushed him onto his stomach. Speedily he cuffed the murderous youth and whipped out his radio to call for backup. All the while Cuckoo grinned as he stared at Bravo.

CHAPTER FOURTEEN

Roe's cell phone rang several times on the nightstand. Wearing only a pair of panties, Felicia was across the room removing five 100 dollar bills from the bankroll she'd taken from Roe's pants pocket. The ringing of the phone made Roe stir and she rushed to rewrap the money in rubber bands and return it to his pocket. She duffed the stolen money in her shoe and hurried over to the nightstand to pick up Roe's phone. She answered it and heard several clicks before the call connected.

"Hello."

"Put Roe on the phone," L.J. commanded.

"Hold on a sec," Felicia said. She reached over and shook Roe's shoulder. "Roe, Roe. Get the phone. Get the phone. It sound like L.J."

Without lifting his head from the hotel room pillow, Roe reached out for his phone. "Yeah?"

"Where you at?"

"Me, Tee and Squeak got some rooms downtown at the Hilton," Roe answered, his voice a bit muffled by the pillow. "Polo got a hookup on rooms."

"Family, I'm gonna need you to take care of somethin' in the mornin' for me."

"What is it?"

"I need you to take them two pies out west to Dee nem, and Congo from over east need a half pie. Charlo said he want an eighth too, but I think he got short bread, so count his bread before you give him anything."

Roe forced himself to sit up. He said, "Damn nigga, you

74

got me running all over the place. Why you or Polo can't do the shit?"

"Nigga, because we can't. We finta be runnin' around all day bonding out fools and looking at some property. It don't make a difference. Take care of that shit for me, Family. Oh yeah, I got a bracelet for you. Nigga sold it to me, but I don't want it. It's more yo' style. Too many diamonds for me."

"Alright, I'm on it in the morning." L.J. ended the call on his end, and before Roe took the phone from his ear, he heard several clicks on the line and then it went dead. He tossed the phone on the bed and looked over at Fefe. She was seated in a chair across from the bed with her legs cocked open, smoking a blunt.

"Come here," Roe said, unwrapping himself from the bed sheet.

She took a deep pull from the blunt and held it in her lungs, before sexily blowing the smoke toward the ceiling. She took another deep hit and held it in again as she left the chair and walked over to the bed. She leaned down like she was going to kiss Roe and blew the weed smoke into his mouth. Felicia handed him the blunt and pushed him backward so he was lying on the bed. She dropped to her knees between his legs and freed him from his boxer shorts.

"You smoke that, while I smoke this," she said sexily, before taking him into her mouth.

With a huge grin on his face, Roe enjoyed Felicia's oral offering as he smoked the blunt.

....

Roe, Squeak and Big Tee were in the lobby of Sand's Subs ordering themselves some food when the door of the restaurant burst open and Cuckoo Carl walked in. He was carrying his Cook County jail property bag and didn't have any shoestrings in his Air Jordans. Polo and L.J. followed him into the restaurant. They all exchanged greetings and hugs before Cuckoo went to the bulletproof window to order some food also.

To the restaurant worker taking the orders, he said, "Aye mothafucka, gimme a gyro, with nacho cheese and gyro sauce only. Don't put shit else on that shit neither. Gyro sauce and American cheese. Salt and pepper on my fries and a grape pop. Don't burn my meat on that grill neither. And please hurry the fuck up! I been eating baloney sammiches for the last coupla days. One of y'all gotta pay for this shit, too. Them slick ass mothafuckas down at the County held the bread I had in my pocket. Said I get a check in four weeks. L.J., Polo, y'all want somethin'?"

L.J. shook his head, but Polo stepped forward, pulling some money out of his pocket. "Gimme a medium steak sub, add grilled onions. Mild sauce on my fries and two orange pops. You sure you on't want shit to eat, L.J.?"

As they ordered, L.J. leaned against the wall with a look of disgust on his face.

"This nigga mad, he don't want shit," Cuckoo said dismissively, as he walked over to Roe and began to tousle with him.

"Fuck you mad for?" Big Tee asked.

L.J. cut his eyes at Cuckoo, who was now trying to put Squeak in a headlock. "Don't even get me started," he said.

Cuckoo released Squeak and said, "Gone 'head and say that shit L.J., say it."

L.J. pushed himself off the wall. He shouted, "You want me to say it? Fuck it, I'm gone say it! Yo' ass shoulda sat in the fuckin County, nigga! We shoulda let yo hard-headed ass sit! Maybe that woulda calmed yo' ass down. Nigga, we down like fifty thousand between bonds and product that got bumped. Thirty gees we wouldn't be out of if you coulda just chilled out like I told you."

"Like you told me? Like you told me, L.J.? I was takin' care of my business like I told you. My job is to protect our shit and that's what I did. You whining about that lil' money like we broke. Nigga, we got enough cash to bond out for 10-20 bodies. That's what the fuck we got money for, Family."

"Well, they don't come before the Family, but them was my homies, too," Roe said. "You didn't have to do the nigga like that neither. Now you owe me the ten gees that I gave to Bravo to get out of town. The police was trying to get him to be on some witness shit, but he kept it gangster. He bounced to his people crib in Virginia."

"I don't give no fuck about that, come get that $10,000 tonight," Cuckoo said nonchalantly. "Anything else?"

"L.J. right Cuckoo," Polo commented. "Here it is you was mad about the heat them niggas brought in a stolen car, so how much heat do you think come with a body? You shoulda left it alone, like we all said. We coulda beat they ass and made them work. You coulda even shot them in they ass or knee or something, but you blow shorty head off? Basically in front of an undercover cop too, that's way wilder than what them niggas did."

"I keep tellin' y'all, it's zero tolerance with me," Cuckoo stated. "That's it, that's all. Fuck up with the Family in any way and I'm comin'. Simple as that. We got plenty of bond money and burners and I'm gone use 'em. This is our shit and if anybody, and I do mean anybody, fuck up what we got going on, they might as well cancel Christmas."

Outside the restaurant, a young couple walked up to the door and pushed it open. They instantly sensed the tension in the lobby and took a quick inventory of the restaurant's occupants, immediately recognizing the street famous members of the Family. The couple mumbled something about suddenly having a taste for Chinese food, and made a swift U-turn. Big Tee kicked the door closed behind them.

L.J. walked over to the bulletproof window and pushed a dollar through the change slot. "Gimme a ginger ale," he said. The worker took the dollar and got a ginger ale pop from the cooler. He put it in the Plexiglas carousel and spun it around. L.J. took the pop and opened it, taking a long swallow. He burped and turned to Cuckoo. In an even voice, he said, "Try to follow what I'm saying nigga, since it's like you don't fuckin' get it. Niggas know what it is with us. We long past them days. Little shit like that happen, but we can't be out here catchin' murders like they speedin' tickets. Ain't nobody try us. Ain't nobody take nothing from us. Cindy and Razo getting knocked come with the game, nigga. That type of shit happen in the game and especially in the projects. All the fuck I'm saying is think."

Behind the glass, the restaurant worker came forward with some of their orders. "What you want on fries? What kind of pop?" he asked Roe, Squeak and Big Tee.

As they were each getting their food in turn, the door burst open and four pre-teen boys walked in.

"Waddup Family? Waddup Roe, L.J, Fat Terrell?" one little boy said.

"Get yo' lil' bad ass outta here," Cuckoo growled at the little guy.

"Nigga, that's my nephew," Roe said. "Bingo, what you up to boy?"

"Shit, unc, we tryna see what's up with the Family," Bingo returned. "We tryna get somethin' to eat, but we ain't got no cash."

"Get what you want," Roe said as he stuffed French fries into his mouth.

The little boy started to walk to the counter and order, but he hesitated. He turned to Roe, "Just me?" he asked.

Squeak stepped forward to pay for their food, but Roe pushed her back as he looked at his nephew. He said, "Yeah, just you. Them might be yo' homies, but they ain't mine. Gone get you somethin', but I ain't feedin' them, they with you, not me."

"I'm straight then, unc," Bingo replied with a serious look on his baby face. "If they can't eat, then I can't eat. You think I can hold five bucks?"

"What you gone buy with five bucks that's gone feed all y'all?' Big Tee asked, through a mouthful of the double steak burger he had started destroying.

"Shid, I'm gone get us some hot meat, chips and Little Debbie's, and we gone go to one of our clubhouses and slam that shit."

L.J. laughed. "Bingo, that's why I love you, Family. You's a real nigga. Who taught you that?"

"My uncle Roe," he answered proudly. "He taught me if one eat, all eat."

"I was just fuckin' with you nephew," Roe said. "Y'all get whatever y'all want."

The boys rushed to the window and started pushing one another as they tried to place their orders. The restaurant worker had gone to the back to get Polo and Cuckoo's food.

Unaware that the shorties were with the Family members when he came back to the counter, the restaurant worker shouted, "Get away from the window! No money, no food! Go now! No free French fries today! Go!"

Squeak went over to the window and banged on the glass. "Aye mothafucka, they with us!"

The worker piped down in a hurry. "Okay, okay. I am sorry. I am Family, too. I do not want any problems. I am Family."

Squeak slid a couple of twenties through the change slot. "Nigga, give they ass what they want, and give the change to him," she said, pointing at Bingo. "And don't be tryna cheat him, neither."

Polo and Cuckoo received their food and they all began to exit the sandwich shop, but before he could leave out L.J. stopped Cuckoo.

"Look, Family, I'm dead serious, you need to chill the fuck out. Cuckoo, we don't need the extra heat on us. Too much heat and we can't eat."

"Alright, alright, L., I got you Family," Cuckoo conceded. "I'm gone lay low, for real for real. I'm fixin' to bite this sammich, take Roe his cash, take a shower and fuck my bitch. I'm gone chill for a few days. That other nigga got a pass, but he needs to stay gone."

"Gimme your word," L.J. said, looking into Cuckoo's eyes.

Cuckoo held his gaze for a moment, then looked away. He said, "On the Family, that's my word. Long as that nigga Bravo ain't tryna be no witness, I ain't gone do shit to him."

Cuckoo offered his hand to L.J. and he shook it. They left the restaurant leaving the excited little boys behind chattering amongst themselves.

CHAPTER FIFTEEN

Roe yawned as he turned onto their block in the projects. He drove into a parking space and shut off the ignition. He exited the vehicle and pocketed his car keys. There was an early morning chill in the air as he looked up and down the block—it was deserted. He pulled his cell phone from his pocket and attempted to place a call, but he wasn't getting any service. He walked over to Cindy Brady's row house and knocked on the door; no one answered. He was just about to go around the side of the block of row houses to the rear courtyard, when Polo drove up and parked behind his car. Roe walked back to the sidewalk as Polo got out of his car with a coffee cup in his hand, looking extremely tired. Roe laughed and pointed at him.

"Damn, Lo, you look like I feel. Where the fuck you been?"

Polo took a gulp of coffee. "I was gamblin' all fuckin' night at the afterhours joint. They tore my ass up as soon as I came through the door. I was up there all night just tryna get some of my fuckin' money back. I swear I'm givin' up this gamblin' shit. I'm for real this time. I throw bricks at the penitentiary every day and then turn around and give it away. That's it for me. Ain't nobody answerin' at Cindy Brady's?"

"Nope," Roe answered. "I tried to call Big Tee or L.J., but I ain't got no service."

"I thought Tee fat ass was with you last night."

"I dropped him off and went to Felicia mama house last night. Her ass be tryna fuck all damn night, Family. I be tellin' her ass I got to get up in the morning."

"What time is it?" Polo asked.

80

"Almost seven. We was here when it was time to open up, so I don't wanna hear L.J.'s mouth. I'm still getting off at three, too. I got shit to do."

Polo said, "Hell yeah, Family. I can't wait to get off. I'm taking my ass straight to sleep. I'm goin' to my bitch crib out south and sleep 'til tomorrow. I know I always say that shit, but my ass is whupped, I need some sleep. Man, this some bullshit, c'mon let's see what the fuck is goin' on. Ain't no security set-up or shit. Try and call Big Tee or L.J. again."

Roe removed his cell phone from the belt holster and pressed redial. He put the phone to his ear, and looked up and down the street as he waited for the call to connect. His eyes grew big as a line of police vehicles turned onto the block.

"Polo! Polo! Look Family, them people deep as hell!"

Polo dropped his coffee at the sight of so many police vehicles and took off. Roe followed him as they sprinted around the side of the row house block and headed for the back courtyard. They ran smack dab into the arms of several federal agents.

"Get down! Get the fuck down! Get on the ground now!" the agents shouted, aiming semi automatic rifles at the pair of boys.

Roe and Polo raised their hands and descended to their knees. The agents swarmed them and pushed them down onto their stomachs, pinning their hands behind their backs with plastic cuffs. One agent removed their wallets and took their IDs out of them. He handed the IDs to an agent that took a piece of paper with a list of names on it from his pocket. Using their IDs as a reference he compared them to the names on the list. He nodded his head.

The agent announced, "This is Pearson and French. I'll inform Tactical HQ that we have them in custody. Get them out of here. Search their vehicles."

The agents pulled them to their feet and walked them back out to the sidewalk. They made the both of them get on their knees, and took their car keys to search their vehicles. They found a gun in Polo's car, which one agent held aloft.

"Gun in French's auto," the agent announced. He ejected the clip and the round in the chamber, before placing it in a plastic evidence bag. "Weapon clear and secured."

"Pearson's auto is clean," another agent called out.

Roe and Polo snuck a glance at one another. The agents pulled them to their feet and signaled for a transport.

"Aye, officer," Polo started.

One of the agents wearing a blue and gold FBI jacket instantly silenced him. "Shut the fuck up, you drug dealing piece of shit. If you've got anything to say, save it for your sentencing hearing."

Several agents within earshot snickered at his remark. An unmarked Ford Crown Victoria drove up and the agents roughly inserted Roe and Polo into the rear of the car. As the car drove off with them, they saw a team of agents bursting into Cindy Brady's row house, and a row house they'd recently been using as a cook house. Roe hung his head, because he knew it was over.

....

No Family Member cooperated with the United States Government, and they were all convicted of the RICO Act as a part of an ongoing criminal enterprise.

Roe received 180 months (15 years) in the Federal penitentiary.

Polo received 180 months (15 years) in the Federal penitentiary.

Big Tee received 180 months (15 years) in the Federal penitentiary.

Frenchie received 300 months (25 years) to Life in the Federal penitentiary.

Martina was deported from the United States to El Salvador.

Cindy Brady received 180 months (15 years) in the Federal penitentiary.

Squeak received Juvenile Life to be released when she was 21 years old.

L.J. received 300 months (25 years) to Life in the Federal penitentiary.

Cuckoo Carl was also convicted of threatening a federal agent, and murdering a government informant (Ice). He received Life without the possibility of parole in the Federal penitentiary, plus 50 years from the state of Illinois.

WHEN I CAME HOME, THE PROJECTS WERE GONE...

CHAPTER SIXTEEN

Three parole board officials sat at a metal, sturdy legged table in a small conference room. The bare concrete block walls were coated in drab, metal gray paint. The only other furniture in the room was a wooden chair positioned directly in front of the assembled panel. The three officials took their time going through a stack of prisoner files. Some of the files they even stamped with a glaringly red PAROLE DENIED stamp without taking the time to actually see the prisoners.

Ms. Harding, a statuesque Black woman with her hair pulled into a severe ponytail, resided over the proceedings. To her left sat Mr. Andie, an overweight, fifty-something, white male with a penchant for chewing tobacco. He was much shorter than Ms. Harding and he often felt like he should challenge her every decision to compensate for his short physical stature. Mr. Andie wasn't a blatant racist, but he wasn't far off. Mr. Taylor, a Black man in his early 30s, seemed to balance the pair out. He was a thoughtful speaker and most times liked to have the solution to a problem before he spoke out about it.

Mr. Andie was about to stamp an inmate's file with PAROLE DENIED when Ms. Harding stopped him. "Mr. Andie, let me see that one before you stamp that."

He handed her the folder. "How many times I gotta tell you, you can call me Bret when no inmates are around, Gwen."

Ms. Harding looked over her reading glasses at Mr. Andie like he was a piece of filth. "No thank you," she said. "I prefer to remain formal at all times. When you become informal, it isn't long before people are becoming too familiar and taking liberties."

She thumbed through the file folder, and made several notes on the yellow legal pad in front of her.

"What's that for?" Mr. Andie asked. "Most of this is a mere formality. These assholes aren't going anywhere but back to their cells."

"Well, this one, Monroe Pearson deserves a closer look. What do you think, Mr. Taylor?"

She slid the file folder in front of Mr. Taylor and waited for him to thumb through it. "Do you see what I'm saying, Mr. Taylor?"

Mr. Andie rolled his eyes. "I think it's a waste of time, but if you want to spend your afternoon interviewing one of these lying, scheming punks then so be it, you're the boss."

Mr. Taylor looked at Ms. Harding. "Yes, you may be right on this one. This guy seems to have done a complete 180. I say let's hear him and then we'll have more to go on. If it's a scam, it's a pretty good one. I'll tell the guard to send him in."

Ms. Harding put her hand on his arm before he could rise from his seat. "Let Mr. Andie do the honors."

Mr. Andie managed to keep a straight face as he waddled over to the door and opened it. To the guard, he said, "Send in Monroe Pearson."

As Mr. Andie regained his seat, Roe walked into the room, he had grown a few inches taller and gained a few pounds, but he still looked exactly the same as when he was a teenager. His prison issued khakis and shirt were immaculate, as was his face bearing only a thin goatee.

"How are y'all doing today?" Roe asked as he took the seat in front of the parole board.

"We're doing fine," answered Ms. Harding. She pointed to her colleagues. "This is Mr. Taylor and Mr. Andie and I'm Ms. Harding. Mr. Pearson, may I call you Monroe?"

"I answer to both," Roe stated simply.

"Well, Monroe," Ms. Harding continued, "my colleagues and I had to take a real good, hard look at your case. I must admit that initially we were ready to deny. Mr. Andie here seemed to be a bit more sympathetic to your cause, and felt that we needed to get you in here to take a closer look at you."

A bit red-faced, Mr. Andie asked, "This is your 3rd time in

front of the board is it not, Mr. Pearson?"

"You know it is, sir. You've been here both times, but they haven't."

"Well," Mr. Andie said. "I was telling Ms. Harding here, I thought we need to take a closer look at your file at this juncture."

"Well," Mr. Taylor started, "in the beginning you have to admit, you were a bit of a wild one, Mr. Pearson. Several assaults."

"Alleged assaults," Roe interjected. "Alleged."

With a smile, Mr. Taylor continued, "Okay, alleged assaults. However, you were repeatedly caught with contraband, everything from tobacco to knives. You've received plenty of insubordination tickets, and you were extremely disruptive whenever you did decide to go to school."

Ms. Harding poured herself a glass of water from the pitcher on the table and took a swallow before zeroing in on Roe. "And then out of nowhere, you seemed to completely change direction, Mr. Pearson. You started taking school much more seriously. As I see here you achieved not only your GED, but you managed to receive a degree in business management and a certificate in culinary arts. You've become a model prisoner, not so much as a blip on the administration's radar in years. I personally don't believe these institutions rehabilitate anyone, so I would love to know what brought about this sudden change, Mr. Pearson?

Roe looked around the room as he ordered his thoughts. After a moment, he said, "I lost my mother awhile back and couldn't even go to the funeral. I lost my cousin while I was in here. The worst part is that if I hadn't allegedly been breaking the rules, I would have been home and could have possibly saved him. The truth is, I miss my family and acting the way I was acting, there wasn't no telling if I was gone see them again."

"When I came here I was a kid, a kid that had seen way too much at a young age. I thought I knew everything, but I didn't know shit, I mean nothing. I had no idea about how things really work in the world. Where I'm from you just had to be the most aggressive and you could make it from day to day. For all intents and purposes, I grew up in here and I'll confess in the beginning I lost my way and was influenced by the wrong people. That isn't an excuse, because that's life I'm guessing, you live and learn and try to do better. It took some time, but I got my mind right."

For a few moments, Ms. Harding locked eyes with Roe, seemingly trying to detect any lies or falsehoods. Unwavering, he met her gaze. Finally, she dropped her eyes as she scribbled something in his file folder.

Mr. Taylor, Mr. Andie, do you have any more questions for Mr. Pearson?" asked Ms. Harding. Both men answered no. "Well, ok, thank you Mr. Pearson. We'll take all of these things into consideration and you'll have this panel's decision in a day or so. Thank you."

Roe stood up. "Well, whatever you decide, thank you for the chance."

Instead of leaving the room, Roe walked forward to the table, which startled Mr. Andie, who looked like he wanted to crawl under the table. The others on the panel looked up at Roe. He stuck out his hand and shook each of their hands in turn. He turned and walked to the door and the guard escorted him from the room.

CHAPTER SEVENTEEN

Roe laid on his bunk with a copy of Y. Blak Moore's DIESEL DOLLS resting on his chest. He called himself reading, but he was actually lost in thought. It had been two and a half days since he'd been to his parole hearing. At first he was optimistic, but as the hours turned into days he began to feel that he'd flopped and he was just waiting on the letter to make it official. He had been denied before so he already knew what the hurt and disappointment felt like. It was different this time though, he had been doing everything he could think of to change things up, to better his chances of release, but he still had his doubts. He also knew he couldn't stand another year or two in this place. He didn't know what he would do if he had to stay any longer.

When he first landed in the federal penitentiary at the ripe old age of 17, he didn't know anything but the street life. In a crazy way, he actually looked forward to being here and maybe meeting a drug lord that would offer him a pipeline of drugs when he got out. Time wasn't relevant to him then and he had no idea just how long 15 years was, since he was so young. He should have paroled to the world in 13 and half years like Cindy Brady, Big Tee and Polo, but because of his actions he'd been here almost three years longer than he should have been.

Like he told the parole board, it had taken the death of his mother and missing her funeral to really wake him up. He had fallen into a deep depression and it was only the wise counsel of an OG named Posey, that helped him get himself together. Posey ran the projects with his father and uncles back in the days and still had over 10 years to go on his sentence. None of his co-defendants were in the same joint as him, so Roe felt like he couldn't trust anyone.

"Pearson," said a guard, standing at his cell door.

Roe looked up at him. "What's up?"

"Here," the guard said, holding a plain white envelope through the bars.

Roe marked his page in the book and laid it on the bunk. He got up and walked over to the bars. As he reached for the envelope the guard pulled it back out of his reach, which he seemed to find really amusing. He extended it to Roe and pulled it back twice, before Roe stopped reaching for it. Losing interest because Roe didn't want to play his game, the guard scowled and tossed the envelope into Roe's cell. He walked away as Roe bent down and picked up the envelope.

"Pussy ass cracker," Roe grumbled as he stood in the middle of his cell. He looked at the envelope, it's only marking was his handwritten name on the front. He opened the unsealed envelope and pulled out the letter; it was from the parole board. He opened the letter and before he read a single sentence, he saw Release Granted stamped in black ink on the letter. A quick read of the letter's contents made him want to jump for joy because he was being released from custody, without parole. His time was considered served in full.

Tears welled up in his eyes as he realized he was finally going home. He had all but given up hope, but deep down inside, he had hoped against all hope that the board would release him. He was going home.

Later that day, as Roe was packing his things so he would be ready to go in the a.m., Posey walked into his house.

"Money Monroe," Posey said, extending his hand for a shake.

Roe took it and gave him a firm handshake and a half hug. "My nigga, Posey," he said with a huge grin on his face. "They done fucked around and let a real nigga up out this bitch."

"Straight up?" Posey asked. "How long you on paper for?"

"Not one damn day big bro. No ink on me, no parole. The federal government is no longer interested in my Black ass."

Posey patted Roe on the back. "Well, I don't know how true it is about them not being interested in you any longer, because it ain't like this place gone close because you free. But fuck all that, I told you if you chill out, they would have to let you out this funky mothafucka. I'm happy for you, Money."

"Thanks, unc," Roe said. "I'm glad you put me up on game, because I wasn't doing nothin' but jaggin' my bit off. I done already gave them people extra time out my life. That shit was goofy as hell."

"Wadn't no thang, nephew. I understand. Me and yo' pops and nems was wild as hell, too. When you touched down you was a baby, but you did yo' time with honor, you just had some lessons to learn. I'm glad I get to see you go to the crib though."

"No disrespect, Posey, but I am too."

Posey took a seat on the metal stool attached to the desk in the cell, and Roe took a seat on his bunk. Posey fingered the chess pieces on the board on top of the desk.

"Roe, don't get out there and forget all the lessons you've learned and the shit I taught you. Just remember the game ain't changed, but the players have. These new niggas is something else. You see damn near everybody that got locked up in the last ten years got some foul paperwork or somebody they really fucked with told on them. Y'all crew was one of the last crews that went down without nobody snitchin'. That shit is damn near unheard of these days."

"Yeah, Posey that is crazy, because we used to get down on snitches, but now they honor these soft ass niggas. I ain't never seen nothin' like this shit. Matter fact, that shit scares me. They can stay away from me with that shit. I'm gone stick to my plan, I don't want no trouble."

Posey knocked over the white king on the chess board and stood up. He said, "You know what it's like out there, nigga. Mothafuckas been coming in here for the last ten years tellin' how fucked up it is. Don't forget that when you get out there. Remember nigga, you seen the direct results of that bullshit out there, so don't go foolin' yourself. You hold it down out there, Family."

"I got you unc, and you gone take that box right there. Thanks again."

Posey picked up the box of food items and toiletries, and shook hands with Roe once more before leaving his cell. Roe returned to his packing, continuing to place his books in another box. He removed his pictures from the wall and packed those, too. One picture in particular he took from the wall with great care. In the picture, he was standing with his four friends, also his co-defendants on the case that landed him in the federal penitentiary. They were at a party at the recreation center in the projects where they grew up. They were so young then, just boys, but the government had pursued them like they were full grown gangsters.

Roe knew that his mind was so different from the teenage version of himself in the picture. He had learned a lot from the mistakes he'd made in his previous life as a teenage hustler and gang member. It was crazy that he'd learned so much about life in prison, but it didn't make a difference where you learned something, as long as you learned it. All he knew was that he was finally headed home. Technically, home didn't exist anymore because the projects had been torn down for years now, but he would cross that bridge when he got there. He tucked the photo in with his belongings and finished packing.

CHAPTER EIGHTEEN

As Polo slowly drove Roe through the mile square area of the city where the place he was born and raised once stood, Roe was awestruck. There was a look of pure disbelief on his face.

He turned to Polo. "Joe, when you said they was gone, I believed you, but I didn't believe you. I mean, in my mind, I was like how could that big ass project really be gone? All of the buildings and row houses, gone. The swimming pool and the whole fuckin Center building is gone, Family. The walk-ups gone. The playgrounds gone. Even the fuckin' stores. Daaaaaaammmmmmnnnn!"

Polo steered slowly around a corner, a corner where they once used to stand as kids and throw rocks at police cars, trying to get the cops to chase them. Now the leasing office for the mixed income housing that replaced the projects stood there. The playground not far from that spot, where Roe had gotten pushed off the slide as a kid and broken his wrist was gone too. The back courtyard of the row houses where they'd made their fortunes was now the parking lot to a senior citizen building.

The heart of Familyland was now $3-400,000 homes with 2 and a half bathrooms, 4 bedrooms, basements, backyards and garages. The strip of land where Sand's Sub Shop, Stein's Liquors, the doctor's office and the laundry mat used to be located were now fenced off vacant lots. The car wash was closed and the liquor stores, barber shops, beauty shops and barbecue joint were nowhere to be seen; so were the gas station and the two motels that used to be located at opposite ends of the projects.

Polo looked over at his friend. "Family, it's gone take some gettin' used to, believe me I know. When I first came home three years ago, I was looking crazy too. A couple of my people got apartments here in the new stuff though, so that helped some."

"Yeah, some of my people do too," Roe said. "My sister and my nephew Bingo. My auntie said Bingo be on bullshit."

Polo nodded his head in agreement. "I know his bad ass. He wild as hell now. Like the shit they be on, I can't even understand. All the little niggas do is break in cribs and cars and get high as hell off them fuckin' pills."

"So is it a lot of niggas from the jets through here?" Roe asked, with a small note of hope in his voice.

Polo burst his bubble. "Not like that, Family. I heard that a lot of people bounced when they started tearing down the buildings. They started moving out of town and takin' Section 8, spreading out around the city and in the 'burbs. Really, mafuckas is everywhere, out west, over east, in the 100s, in Englewood, by 63rd, in the 50s. Some people did move back though. On warm days a lot of people come hang out in the park where our grammar school was. It be deep right there sometimes. Holidays and days like after the Bud Billiken parade"

As they drove past the spot where his favorite restaurant once stood, Roe sounded sad when he said, "Damn, Joe, even the restaurant is gone. I would have loved a gyro or Italian beef out that bitch. This some cold-blooded shit, fam. Cold than a mothafucka."

"Don't worry 'bout that, Roe, them Arabs ain't gone nowhere. It's one on Ashland, and the other is on 69th."

"The same Arabs? I bet the shit don't taste the same."

"It do, Family. Or as close to it as we gone get. I'm gone run you out there, let you get yo' gyro on."

Polo pulled over in the parking lot of the new shopping center, which had been built where the east side of the projects once stood. They sat quietly and Roe watched the people coming and going as they shopped at the stores.

"Man, what the fuck happened with Big Tee?" Roe asked quietly, breaking their silence. "All I know is Cindy Brady was sending me these long ass letters quoting the bible, then she told me he got killed. What happened to him, Lo?"

"Joe, that nigga was with Squeak on 62nd. He went out there with them niggas and had them gettin' money. Had they ass soldierin', too. I gave the nigga 25 grams of heroin and he never looked back. He just started going up and up, before I knew it he was copping half a key of dope. He was gettin' too much money, and them niggas tried to tax him, but he wasn't goin'. He got into one of them block beefs. Squeak told me he ended up killin' a couple of they guys and then they killed him. Squeak and her guys been going nuts for him every since. Speaking of Cindy Brady, she lookin' for you. She say she got somethin' for you."

"I don't wanna hear none of that religious shit, Polo. She can gone with that. I done a lot of reading in the joint and I don't believe none of that shit no more. I ain't tryna hear none of that shit, and you bet not tell her that I'm over Big Tee mama crib neither. I ain't playin' neither Polo."

Polo smiled. "You gotta see Cindy Brady, Roe. She all healthy and shit. She still wear blonde hair though, but it look better than them wigs she used to have on. When she do see you, she is gone damn near pray yo' ass to death. Oh shit, you gotta see yo girl Fefe too, Family. That bitch is whupped. She a beer drinkin' ass bitch now. She think she thick, but her ass fat as hell."

"For real?" Roe asked, slightly interested. "She fat now?"

"As hell! She ended up gettin' pregnant by some nigga that was whuppin' her ass and puttin' babies in her. She was up in the 'Sota Pop for some years. She got like five or six shorties. The nigga she was with end up gettin' killed and her ass been back out here every since. Straight Section 8 pussy. The few times I bumped into her in the club or somewhere, she was talkin' that she can't wait til her baby Money Roe come home shit."

"She better gone with that shit," Roe said. "I ain't on none of that. Joe, that bitch ain't send me a dime while I was down. Not a picture, a visit or even accept a phone call. Fuck her and anybody that look like her. I had a few gees at her crib when we got bagged, too."

"Yeah, well that shit gone, Family," Polo assured him.

"Fuck her though, you need to holla at Rhonda."

"Nigga, Rhonda ain't tryna to talk to me after the way I shitted on her back in the days. I know she ain't gone let me see my daughter neither."

"I done already talked to her, Roe. She ain't on none of that. She really on some cool shit, for real, Family."

"Some cool shit? Did you see what she did to my Chevy back in the days?"

Polo laughed. "Yeah, she did fuck yo' Brougham up. But for real, she said yo' daughter wanna meet you. Rhonda married, too. She gave me her number and said to give it to you, so you can set up a chance to meet Malika."

"Man, I done missed this girl whole life," Roe lamented. "I don't even know how to start off. What the fuck do you say to your own child that you've never met before?"

"How 'bout hi, I'm your daddy," Polo offered. "Ain't shit you can do about the time you missed, just make sure you don't miss no more. Just try to connect with her. I had to do the same shit with my sons when I came home. It might even be easier for you because she's a girl. When I first came home, my sons was angry, Family. They wasn't tryna hear shit, they felt like I had abandoned them and wasn't no tellin' them different. For a minute I was finta say fuck it, but I knew it wasn't they fault and I kept at it and we not the best, but we pretty good now. Give her a call, she cool. I'm tellin' you it's all good, Family."

"I'll call her when I get a phone. I ain't got no phone."

"Stop it Roe, that ain't never about to be yo' excuse. We finta go get you one right now when I take you shopping. I got like five gees for yo' pocket, too. You gone get yourself together and go see yo' daughter, and that's that. You done faced killers and dealers every day for years, you ain't never scared of no little kid. First things first though, you need a real fuckin' haircut, because tonight we goin' out and get you some pussy."

"Now you finally said some shit I wanted to hear," Roe commented. "Let's get from through here because all this new and pretty shit is depressing."

Polo laughed as he started the car. "Yeah, same thing I said. Ain't nothin' like the smell of asbestos, lead paint, funky crackheads and pissy hallways to let you know you at home."

CHAPTER NINETEEN

Rhonda stood in the lobby of Dave and Buster's on North Clark Street drinking a beer. She was casually dressed in a Chicago State University sweatsuit with her hair pulled into a long ponytail. She finished her beer and placed the bottle on a nearby table. She went to the door and peered out of it for a few moments, with her arms folded across her chest. Finally, she turned and was about to go back upstairs to the game room.

Outside D&B's, a Hyundai Santa Fe pulled to the curb in the valet area and deposited Roe on the curb. He spotted Rhonda heading for the escalator and he rushed through the revolving doors.

"Rhonda! Rhonda," Roe called out.

She turned at the sound of her name and gave him a blank look. Then her face brightened. She said, "I thought you wasn't gonna make it, Monroe. I would have hated to tell your daughter that."

Roe smiled bashfully at the sound of his government name. "Damn, you just gone throw a nigga government name around like that? Don't do that baby mama, call me Roe."

Rhonda laughed as she continued on the escalator. "Boy, you better gone, I ain't calling you Roe. I ain't one of your fans. I been calling you Monroe since 3rd grade, and I ain't about to stop now. And don't call me baby mama, I'm a married woman. Just call me Rhonda and we'll get along just fine."

"My bad, my bad," Roe apologized as he raised his hands in mock surrender. "It won't happen again. Sorry, it took so long, that goofy ass Uber driver kept gettin' lost."

"Long as you here now, that's all that matters," Rhonda said as they got off the escalator on the second level. "Let's go inside to the bar for a moment."

Roe looked around nervously, he was sweating and looked a bit queasy. "Is she there?" he asked in a voice just above a whisper.

"No, she's by the games. You act like you ain't never been here before."

"I haven't. I was in prison," Roe said, after taking a deep breath.

For the first time, Rhonda noticed his nervousness. "She's just a 16-year old girl, you've faced worse. To answer your question, she's not at the bar. She's in the game room. This is her favorite place, so I was thinking it would be a good meeting place for you two. She wants her father in her life, and I'm guessing you want to be there, or you wouldn't have called. You reaching out and making it here today says a lot about your intentions. Just so you know, her life is good without you, so with you it should only be better, right?"

Roe nodded his head, following Rhonda into the bar area. She ordered herself a beer.

Rhonda continued, "My advice is take your time, let her come to you. Don't do too much, as the kids say. No pressure, eat some food, play a few games and talk a little. C'mon, you ready?"

"As ready as I'm ever gonna be," Roe replied.

Rhonda laughed as she got her beer from the bartender. "I can't believe this. Bad ass Roe from the Family, ain't scared of shit, but you shook to meet your teenage daughter."

"Ain't nobody scared, let's go," Roe said, hoping that he sounded confident.

"Say no more," Rhonda said.

They left the bar area and went into the arcade. They walked around the numerous video games until they spotted Malika. She was playing a dancing game with a little Chinese girl and they were going at it. Both of her parents stood and watched the girls, waiting for them to finish. When their game was over, Malika hugged the girl and hopped down off the dance pad. Her face was flushed as she looked around for another game to play.

"Malika, come here for a second," Rhonda called to her.

Malika skipped over to her mother, never taking her eyes off Roe the entire way.

"Hey, Ma," Malika said.

"Hey baby you having fun?"

"Yeah, Ma," Malika answered, still staring at her father.

"Malika, this is your father," Rhonda announced. "He came to meet you today."

Malika didn't do or say anything for a moment, except lock eyes with Roe. He braced himself for what he felt would be forthcoming hostilities, but instead her pretty brown face broke into a mile-wide grin as she showed her teeth with lime green braces on them.

"Waddup Pops, how you doing?" she said.

Her bright smile made Roe smile, too. He replied, "I guess, I'm doing pretty alright now that I see you."

"That's wassup! Well, give your girl a hug," Malika said, while holding her arms open wide. "Get on in here."

As they embraced for the first time in both of their lives, Roe felt like he finally had a part of him that had been missing for years. Rhonda got a little misty-eyed looking at the expression of love on her daughter's face as she hugged her father.

"Alright, that's enough you two, break it up, people are starting to stare."

Roe and Malika released their embrace, but they stayed near one another. Roe looked her deep into her brown eyes. He said, "Baby girl, my family made sure that I had some pictures of you over the years, but them pictures ain't do you justice. You're beautiful."

Malika blushed as she pulled her cell phone from her back pocket and handed it to her mother. She slipped her arm around her dad's waist. "Ma, take a picture of us, so I can put it up on Snapchat."

"Okay, then we're going to eat. Man, I didn't realize just how much y'all look alike." She took several pictures of her daughter and Roe then handed the phone back to Malika so she could inspect them. "Alright, I'm about to get a booth and order some food. I already know, Malika, you want Buffalo wings and loaded fries. What about you, Monroe?"

"I don't know, let me ask the person whose favorite place this is. What should I get Malika? What's good?"

"As a rule, Pops, you can pretty much never go wrong with Buffalo wings and loaded fries. Also make sure you get blue cheese, ranch is for suckers."

"Let me go put this order in," Rhonda said, rolling her eyes. "You two don't get lost."

"Let's go kill some zombies, Pops," Malika suggested. "There's this boss on the third level that I can't get past. Hopefully, you can shoot, Pops."

"Well, I don't know about killing zombies, but point me toward them and it's on."

"Pops, all you gotta do is aim, shoot and reload. You gonna like it, watch."

She grabbed his arm and pulled him over to the zombie killing game. She swiped her card and soon they were in combat. They killed wave after wave of zombies, even managing to beat the zombie boss that had given Malika so much trouble in the past. Eventually, they lost after depleting Malika's game card. As they stepped back from the game to give a couple that were waiting for a chance to play the game, Malika looked at her cell phone.

""Dag, Pops you about to get us in trouble. My mama done text me three times. C'mon before she starts tripping. She said the booth right over there by the ramp. Pops, you gonna learn you have to be on time dealing with my mama. That's one of her pet peeves. OG trips when you're late."

Malika and Roe jogged over to the booth and took a seat. They weren't in trouble yet because their food hadn't arrived, but it did shortly after they were seated. Buffalo wings, loaded French fries and Rhonda's favorite, chicken quesadillas covered the table. As Roe dug into the wings and fries, he realized how hungry he was because he hadn't eaten since breakfast, and he had only picked over it at that.

As they ate, they talked and joked, father and daughter taking turns stealing wings from one another. When they were finished eating, Roe and Malika were about to leave the table to go play more games, when Rhonda put her hand on his arm.

"Malika, you go on ahead and play some games while I

talk to your father," Rhonda said.

"Ain't nothing left on my card, Ma. Can I get like 20 bucks?"

Rhonda took her debit card from her phone case. "Damn, girl I just put $20 on that damn card, you better take your time, because that's it. $20 only and bring me my debit card before you start playing them games."

Nonchalantly, Roe pulled a bankroll from his pocket. He counted out $100 and handed it to Malika. "Go put that on the card," he said as he returned his money to his pocket. He looked up into Rhonda's stern face and Malika's excited face.

"The whole thing?" Malika asked breathlessly. "All of it?"

Roe looked away from Rhonda, he smiled at Malika. "Yeah, baby. Put it all on there. We about to game out. I'm trying to win you a teddy bear or somethin'. You gone 'head, I'm right behind you. I'm finta see what yo' OG, I mean yo' mother is talkin' about." As Malika ran off to load the money on her card, Roe faced an irritated Rhonda. "Damn, Rhonda, what the fuck I do? I was just trying to make sure we have a good time. This is the first time I'm really meeting my daughter."

"You just don't get it Monroe," she said angrily. "Obviously from the amount of money you're carrying around, you're back up to your old tricks. I don't want my daughter's heart broke if something happens to your ass, and don't start spoiling her. Don't do nothing for her that you can't keep up, I don't have time for that shit. What the fuck you think is going to happen if you go away again? I gotta deal with that. I don't want my baby hurt, Monroe."

Roe raised his glass and signaled to the server for another beer. She hurried over and took his glass, while making sure to maintain eye contact with him.

"What's your name cutie?" Roe asked smoothly.

"Erika, with a k," she replied, licking her tongue along her teeth.

"Well, Erika with a k, me and my child's mother here would like another beer please. You think you can do that for me?"

"Absolutely, say no more, they're on the way."

The waitress walked away looking back over her shoulder at Roe, who was unashamedly checking out her very nice butt.

"Um, um, um," Roe said. "That girl got a future behind her!"

"Monroe, you're seriously going to flirt with the waitress while I'm talking to you about our daughter?"

"Hell yeah, I'm tryna come up. I just got out of prison. I'm tryin' to take shit down out here. Shid, if you wasn't married with children, I'd be trying to bag you. I ain't forgot that was my coochie."

Rhonda almost spit out the beer she was sipping. She picked up a napkin and wiped her mouth. "You got that shit backward, boy. I took yo' virginity, you ain't take mine. That was my dick 'til you started giving it to all the hoodrats. You know what, I'm not even about to revisit that bullshit, because it don't have nothin' to do with nothin'. Like I said, Monroe, please do not bullshit my child. Don't get her all spoiled and loving her daddy and then you gone again for another 20 years. You not about to hurt my baby like that."

"Well," Roe said. "First off it wasn't 20 years, damn near, but it wasn't. Secondly it ain't like I was trying to get locked up. I was young and dumb, but I'm grown as hell now. You may not believe me, but I really have changed and I won't do nothing to take me out of my daughter's life again, if I can help it. Now you said on the phone that you was gone trust me, so let me at least fuck up before you start acting like I did."

Several times Rhonda started to speak, but she stopped and thought about it. Finally, she said, "You know what, Monroe? You're right. I'm going to give you a fair shot at being a father to your daughter. I said that's what I was going to do so that's what I'm going to do."

"Well good, so could you shut up with the 'our kid' stuff when this sexy ass waitress comes back over here," Roe said from the side of his mouth as the waitress approached with their beers.

The waitress put the beers on table, all the while smiling at Roe. He gave her a generous tip, making sure to touch her hand and look her in the eye. Erika walked away with a huge smile on her face and kept looking back at Roe, almost succeeding in colliding with a group of excited children running through the arcade.

It was Rhonda's turn to roll her eyes. When Roe was focused again, she said, "I do want to ask you one question. How was your relationship with your mother when she passed? Did she ever attempt to straighten things out with you before she, you know, died?"

Roe looked away from Rhonda with obvious pain in his eyes. He said, "Nall, we never got a chance to, either of us. When she knew she had AIDS and it was basically a hit, she tried to reach out to me, but I was too immature to forgive her. I couldn't see past my anger and I blamed her for all of my mistakes. I mean, she was a dopefiend, she fucked up our childhood. Big Tee momma, Martha, my auntie Carly and Cindy Brady raised me and my brothers and sisters. I can't say if I'll ever get past those regrets, but then again, I don't know that I want to try."

"Yeah, it sounds like it took a toll on you," Rhonda admitted. "To tell you the truth I never even gave it too much thought, until Malika started wondering about her other grandmother. At first, I didn't know what to tell her, but soon after your mother died, I told her the truth. I'm sorry about her passing and I wish y'all would have gotten a chance to mend y'all fences."

"Look, Rhonda, I'm through talkin' about it," Roe said, a bit more irritably than he felt. He reached into his pocket and pulled out some money. He counted out $1000 and dropped it on the table in front of Rhonda.

She didn't touch the money—just looked at it. "What's that for? I didn't ask you for any money? That wasn't what this was about. My daughter doesn't have a price tag."

Roe sighed. "Look, I'm not trying to buy my daughter's love, if I got some money, I'm gone break bread with you and her. The way I look at it, I owe you for taking care of her for all these years and you know I don't like owing nobody shit. She's my kid, and I want to help take care of her. I'll make sure if nothing else, I got her from this day on. Prom, graduation, college, all that good shit. I'm not goin' nowhere."

Both parents locked eyes. Roe looked down at the money and back at Rhonda. Defiantly, Rhonda still didn't claim the cash.

"That's okay, I'm just gone give it to her," Roe said, as he made a move for the money.

"Oh, hell naw!" Rhonda squawked, sweeping the cash up. She tucked it away. "That girl already starting to smell her ass, and you think you about to give her a thousand reasons why? Hell the fuck no! You got me fucked up."

Roe stood up and drained his beer. He placed the empty bottle on the table. "Thank you. Well, now I'm going to kill zombies or whatever with the new love of my life, but I'm also going to make sure I get a number from a certain waitress, because I'll be clappin' those cheeks later."

Rhonda shook her head. "You gone ahead, crazy man. I'm gonna need another beer after this."

Grinning, Roe walked toward the arcade; he spotted Malika coming his way. When she spotted him, she ran into his arms and gave him a huge embrace. He returned her hug.

Malika led him by the hand as she looked up at him and said, "I was just coming to rescue you, Pops. I know my mama can be real intense. Now, let's go over here, I found the game that's gonna give us enough tickets for me to win that big, furry gorilla."

"What you want with a gorilla?" he asked.

"I'm gonna name it Pops and keep it for forever. Just because it reminds me of you."

Roe smiled, "Well, like Ice Cube said, if you gotta be a monkey, you might as well be a gorilla."

"Pops, Ice Cube might have been lit back in the 60s, but please don't mention him again," Malika said. "Now c'mon, we finta get these tickets."

CHAPTER TWENTY

Roe's eyes popped open and he looked at the unfamiliar ceiling. He knew he wasn't still in the penitentiary because he knew every inch, every crack and every spider web on the ceiling of the cell he had called home for years. He knew it wasn't the ceiling of Big Tee's bedroom at his Aunt Martha's house. He'd been staying there since he got out of prison a couple of weeks ago. Slowly he peeked around the room and his Hennessey soaked memory came flooding back.

As a stream of pre-dawn light peeked into the bedroom, Roe looked around the room. It was a cluttered mess, with clothes and shoes strewn everywhere. He sat up as fast as the previous night's drinking would allow and looked over at his bedmate. Erika, the waitress from Dave & Buster's was face down snoring lightly into her pillow. He pulled the sheet back and had to once again give a nod of approval to her very generous portion of ass. He'd spent the better part of the night clapping those heavenly cheeks.

He thought that maybe he would have to take Erika on several dates, pay for some expensive dinners, and spend a couple of hours on the phone to hit it, but it didn't require any of that. After Rhonda left with Malika, he sat at the bar drinking shots of Hennessey while he flirted with her. When her shift was over, she suggested they take an Uber to her apartment in the South Loop. Judging from the building's swanky look, he had no way of knowing she was such a poor housekeeper. He wasn't there to judge her homemaking skills anyway, so in no time at all, she was on her knees letting him take a tour of her tonsil game. He had worked her out pretty good, and they both passed out on the clothes covered bed in her untidy bedroom.

Just thinking about her wet pussy made his dick rise. He reached over and rubbed between her legs, until she moaned and rolled onto her back, spreading her legs. Roe forced a condom onto his dick and straddled her. Soon they were going at it like this would be the last time either of them had sex. He let her climb on top and she rode him until she orgasmed. She was still gasping for breath when he pushed her off of him and positioned her on the edge of the bed with her glorious ass in the air. He gripped her hips, and powerfully plunged his morning stiffness into her fat pussy from the back until he drained his sacs into the condom. Spent, Roe sagged onto the bed and panted as he caught his breath. Erika stayed in the same position with her back arched and her ass in the air for a few more moments, before collapsing beside him on the bed.

"Damn, what time is it?" she asked, her voice somewhat muffled by the pillow.

"Almost six," Roe answered.

"What the fuck you doing up so damn early, man?"

"I always get up early," Roe replied, thinking about how early breakfast was served in prison. "For years now."

"Shid, not me. If I ain't gotta be nowhere, I'm not trying to get out the bed before afternoon. That morning shit is overrated. You sound like my granddaddy with that. His ass used to get up early as hell. How old are you?"

"I'm 'bout to be 34," Roe replied, almost as if he didn't believe it himself.

"What?" Ericka said as she sat up and pulled the bed sheet around her nakedness. "You ain't never finta be 34, nigga! My daddy ain't nothing but 39. Uuuuuhhhhhhh, I just fucked a old head! Nigga, you had yo' old ass dick in my mouth and all in me. I can't believe this shit!"

Roe sat up. "How I'm old? Girl, your ass gotta be 30, 32."

"Nigga, you tweaking! I just made 22, two months ago. I mean the dick was lit and you eat pussy like a champ, but you too old for me to be fuckin' with unless you got some money. I ain't one of these $40 bitches, I make that in tips. So what you gonna do, Pops?"

"Fuck you mean, what I'm gonna do?" Roe asked

indignantly.

"I mean, you about to grab you a Uber or what, old head? I'm trying to get me some sleep." To emphasize her point, Erika crawled up into bed and sank her head onto her pillow. "Just slam the door, it'll lock."

Roe was so shocked at her actions, he couldn't even get too mad as he got dressed. He snatched the rubber full of cum off and dropped it into her purse. He called for an Uber and left the apartment to wait for it. By the time his Uber pulled up, he was worked up though. He had to admit she had slightly bruised his ego. He got in the car, and talked the driver's ears off, a Panamanian man named Breano, about how Erika had just dismissed him because of his age.

At home, he let himself into his Aunt Martha's apartment. He went to the kitchen to get a bottle of water and saw his aunt was at the kitchen table, drinking a cup of coffee, eating a piece of cheese Danish and scrolling through Facebook. He hugged her from the back and kissed her on her jaw. She fanned her hand.

"Boy, you smell just like the liquor store," Martha commented. "Been drinkin' that damn Hennessey again. That shit stank."

Roe grunted as he took a seat at the kitchen counter next to her; he was still looking salty.

"What's wrong with you Money Roe?" Martha asked, without looking up from Facebook.

"Nothin' Auntie, just had a long night."

"Seems like more than a long night. I ain't seen you looking this crazy since yo' mama stole y'all new outfits the night before the Bud Billiken parade. Boy you was tight then, and that's how you look now. What really happened?"

Roe looked down at his water bottle and began to peel the label. He blurted out, "This young bitch called me old, Auntie."

His aunt looked at him for a moment, and then burst into laughter. She laughed so long and loud, that Roe got even more upset, only for a second or two, and then he joined in along with her.

"Nigga, if you coulda seen yo' face when you said that," Martha said, as she wiped the tears away at the corner of her eyes. "She shole took a poop in your pocket with that one. But you gotta realize, to these kids, you is old. When you was a kid...wait a minute, just how young?"

"Really Auntie? I don't see nothin' sexy about no kid, she was 22."

Martha put her hand on her chest. "Well ok, let a bitch know somethin'. I can't have no pedophiles around this place. Well, like I was saying, when you was a youngin', a mothafucka yo' age was old as hell. Yeah, Money, you been gone for a minute. Them prisons be having niggas lookin' young as hell, but some time be done passed. Maybe it's the food, but I personally think it's because it ain't no bitches in there to stress y'all the fuck out everyday."

Roe was silent because he'd heard this conversation before. To him being in the joint felt like being put on pause while the rest of the world kept on moving. He sat there for a while before he asked, "Auntie, do you miss it?"

"Miss what?" Martha asked.

"The projects," Roe said as he looked at his aunt intently.

She pursed her lips and thought about the question carefully. "Some days more than others," she answered wistfully. "Some days I miss every damn thing about that place, and then there's times I hate I ever set eyes on the place. Some beautiful ass people lived there, and some piece-a-shit ass mothafuckas lived there, too. Nigga, I learned good and bad habits there. Got a lotta love and felt a lot of hate there. Yeah, I miss it, 'cause there's no place like home, and there are days I miss it so much it makes me mad and sad."

"I miss that place so much it's scary, Auntie. I be wishin' I dreamt all this shit and I'm gone wake up on Cindy Brady couch, high or drunk from the night before. I wish for that shit, but the reality is the projects gone, Terrance dead, L.J. got another 13-14 years to go, and Carl ain't never comin' home. That nigga gotta die and come back and do 50 years."

"Well," his aunt said, while shaking her head "I'm glad the rest of y'all out, but that damn Carl was a fuckin' serial killer. Every since he was little, I knew he was gonna be the worst of y'all. That nigga would kill a puppy."

Roe didn't laugh at her observation, instead a few tears rolled down his face. "Auntie, I really miss Tee, I was lookin' forward to seein' my cousin. I ain't seent him since I was 17. I would have never thought he would be dead now."

"Yeah, his ass went out there with Squeak lil' crazy self and they turnt that neighborhood upside down. Last time he came here, he was talking about how he be knockin' niggas the fuck out on 63rd. He had started makin' some money again. He was sellin' that damn dope, and all he could talk about was how fast the money came in. He was sittin' right here. Squeak was with him. She was high as organic fruit, and she had a gun damn near bigger than her. Them two sat here and ate up all my greens, mac and cheese and baked chicken. Tee was complainin' that all his bitches can't cook, and Squeak was sayin' she wouldn't have no girl that can't cook. You ain't get to see him Roe, but that nigga had got cocky as hell. He was big for real. What you need to do is go check on Squeak, she was hurt as hell behind Terrance gettin' killed. I ain't seen her but twice since the funeral, but she call me all the time and send me money."

Roe stood up and wiped his face with one of the Burger King napkins on the countertop. He sounded miserable as he said, "Yeah, I'm gone pull up on Squeak. I miss my family, too. I gotta get some sleep first though Auntie. Thanks for the talk."

Roe turned to go to his bedroom, but Martha stopped him. "This may help you, or it may not nephew. It's not your fault with what happened to Tee, he led his own life. I had to tell Squeak that. As far as the projects being gone, they gone. Ain't too much you can do about that. And that can't be the end of things because we gotta keep living. Just say a prayer for the livin' and the dead and keep walkin' your path until your time comes."

"Thanks, Auntie. You have a good day at work," Roe said with his head down. "Love you, I'm going to get some sleep."

CHAPTER TWENTY-ONE

Squeak peeked through one of the holes drilled in the piece of wood that covered the building entrance door of the two-flat Greystone building. As she did, her long dreads swung into her tattooed face. She tucked the gun she was holding into the waistband of her jeans, and tied her dreads into a big knot to keep them out of her face. She pushed outward on the board and slid through the opening. On the porch, she looked up and down the block before walking down the steps to sidewalk level. Two buildings north of her boarded up building, three members of her gang sat on the porch of the building there. She walked over to them and took a seat on the porch amongst them, after showing each of them love.

Her guy named Lil Fuji said, "Squeak the Freak, what's up with it, my nigga?"

"Shit, Family, just came outside to get some air and to watch for my cousin pulling up," Squeak answered, pulling a sandwich baggie with weed in it from her pocket. She tossed the baggie and a pack of blunts to Martell, another one of the young men sitting on the porch. "Put a few of those together, Family. I gotta make sure when my cuddy pull up, don't none of you trigger happy niggas buck at him thinking he a opp."

"Look at that," her friend Parlay said, pointing to a Mazda SUV parked down the block. "We went and took that last night. We gone use that to go put some pressure on the opps later. I'm trying to smoke two, three of they ass for the big homie Terrible. They done got comfortable too, just like you said Freaky Squeaky, if we lay off for a few days. We on they ass tonight though."

"I'm goin' with y'all tonight," Squeak said. "I needs me some action. I ain't been on shit since we caught them bitch ass niggas comin' out the gas station a coupla weeks ago and laid they ass down."

"Yo' ass ain't going," her friend named Pita said. "Family, yo' ass finta be right in the crib, chillin' with Tasha, good smellin', good cookin' ass."

"Did this nigga just say 'good smellin'?" Martell asked, as he stopped rolling the wood. "Freaky, you better keep this nigga away from Tasha, he sneakin' smells and shit."

"I ain't gone have to kill Pita, he know better than that," Squeak assured Martell. "Ain't that right, Pita?"

"Hell nall, I'm talking about when her thick ass walk by all you smell is Chanel perfume, pancakes and pot roast, mothafucka," Pita replied.

They all laughed. Though they were joking amongst themselves, they never stopped watching their surroundings.

"Aye y'all, on this car, it's slowing down," Lil Fuji warned. He pulled a Glock from his hoodie and held it alongside his leg. Squeak put her hand on her gun and Pita edged a bit closer to the Draco in the grass near his feet.

The car, a Chrysler 200 with obvious Uber markings neared to the curb and parked in front of Squeak's building; Roe exited the Uber. Squeak immediately relaxed.

"Y'all stand down, that's my cuddy," Squeak told them, with a big ass smile on her face. She called out, "Roe, check it out, Family."

Roe couldn't hold back his smile either as he walked over to greet his younger cousin. They hugged for a quite a while, as they grinned at one another.

"Man, OG it's good to see you, cuddy. You lookin' good too, Family. You got yo' weight up. Aye, y'all this my cousin Roe, Roe this Pita, Lil Fuji, Martell and Parlay. They all Family. Come show my cuddy some love."

One by one, they all greeted Roe and returned to their positions.

Roe said, "Damn, Squeak. I ain't seen you in real life since we was kids. And the first picture you sent me, you ain't have no ink on your face or dreads. You had braids."

Squeak pointed to the word Terrible, tattooed along her

hairline. "This for our cuddy, Big Tee. Got some ink for a few more of the Family that fell over the years, too. Shit real out here, Family. Roe, you thought the jets was bad, these blocks way worse to me. I'm standing on that. In the projects, you usually knew where shit was coming from. Out here, on these blocks, man a mothafucka will leave you and yo' people won't know why and might not never know. Unless some lame go online, tryna to get some clout for yo' body."

"It's that bad?" Roe asked.

"Hell yeah," answered Pita. "I know you don't 'member me, but I come from the Houses, too. We used to fight against Squeak nem on some grammar school classroom against classroom shit. We got cool when we ended up out here on these blocks. The difference is, as bad as the Houses were, it didn't feel like this. It feel like there ain't no love in these streets and never will be. We Family, so we feel like we all we got out here in the world. That's why we go so hard for each other. Right or wrong."

Roe shook Pita's hand. "That's how we carried it in the joint. You couldn't touch nobody that was jammed with us, we wasn't tryna hear nothin'."

Lil Fuji upped his gun and pushed past them. Watching a car coming up the street, he said, "Y'all look out. I don't know who car this is."

The car rode past without incident and Lil Fuji put his gun away.

"We need to get from out here," Squeak announced. "I'm tryna get high and kick it with my cuddy. I'll be sick if some lame ass opp slide through here and score. I'm killin' everybody after that. Roe, we inside with it. My girl cookin' too, I got bottles. You feel like teein' up with me for old time sakes?"

"I'll do what I can, but I ain't poppin no pills or shit," Roe replied.

Squeak laughed. She said, "Well, I'm gone take a trip to Paris when I pop mine, you stay in Chiraq if you want. Grab that Draco out the grass, Pita."

The group traversed the couple of yards to Squeak's building. Martell pulled the plywood back and they all slid through the crack one by one. Roe halfway expected the place to be condemned, but the hallway was clean—no urine smell or trash on the floor. They trooped up the stairs to the apartment on the second floor. Squeak unlocked several deadbolts and let them inside the apartment. To Roe's surprise, the older apartment had been remodeled to an open floor plan with exposed brick walls, shiny hardwood floors, and a huge kitchen island. In the living room, the furniture was new and there was a colossal television mounted to the wall.

Pita, Lil Fuji, Martell and Parlay shucked their shoes and took seats in the living room, immediately turning on the video game console. Squeak indicated for Roe to remove his shoes too as she was pulling off her Tims. Roe kicked off the Gucci shoes Polo bought him a couple of days ago, and followed Squeak into the kitchen to meet her woman. On the marble kitchen counter, Vanessa was frying chicken in a double basket deep fryer. On the stainless steel stovetop, several pots were cooking, and a muffin pan of freshly baked corn muffins rested there. Vanessa was a short, brown-skinned well-built woman. Her short wavy hair, framed her heart-shaped face perfectly. Squeak wrapped her arms around Vanessa from the back and kissed her on the neck.

"Bae, this my cuddy, Roe, I been tellin' you about," Squeak said. "Roe, this my wife to be Vanessa."

Roe held out his hand. "Nice to meet you," he said.

Vanessa knocked his hand down and gave him a hug. In a Southern drawl, she said, "I don't shake hands family. It's really good to finally meet you. Squeak told me so much about you, I feel like I know you already. I hope that you're sticking around for dinner."

"Oh, most definitely," Roe assured her. "Especially the way you got it smellin' in here."

"You drinkin' light or dark, cuddy?" Squeak asked Roe. She released Vanessa and walked to the dining area where there was a high wooden table with benches. On the table was a box of dominoes and several packs of playing cards. She took her gun out of her waist band and put it on the table. Vanessa walked from the kitchen, picked up Squeak's gun and put it on a placemat and returned to cooking. Against one wall of the dining area was a bar with various bottles of alcohol on the glass top.

"You already know I drink dark."

Squeak picked up a bottle of D'usse. "Ok, well I'm out of Henny, so it's D'usse and lemonade." She took a RAW weed rolling tray with an ashtray and some already rolled Backwoods blunts on it and placed it on the table. They both took a seat at the table and Squeak poured them both a drink. "I usually be drinkin' lean, but I had a seizure like two weeks ago, so I promised Vanessa, I would chill, no pouring up for a little minute."

"A seizure?" asked Roe.

"Hell yeah, cuddy. That was some scary shit. If Vanessa wasn't here I don't know what woulda happened. Them goofy ass niggas up there was hollering and running 'round with they heads cut off. Vanessa made sure I ain't swallow my tongue or hit my head. It was time for me to slow up anyway; I was pourin' a six in a one-liter and was still barely gettin' high. I was in the hospital for like four days, then I came home. I had a few little withdrawals, so I'm just now feelin' betta."

"Dinner will be ready in a few minutes," Vanessa declared. "I'm making your favorite too, bae; peach cobbler."

Squeak grinned. "Man, cuddy, you popped out on the right night. Her mothafuckin' cobbler be bussin'."

"I know! It smell good as hell," Roe said. "But seriously, Squeak, what was up with Big Tee? What happened with cuz?"

At Roe's question a storm cloud crossed Squeak's face. At first her voice was a bit tight, when she said, "Out here we call that nigga Terrible, Money Roe. Tee was a mafucka, cuddy. When he came home, he was cockier than a bitch. I'm talkin' about all fat was gone, that man was strong like a mafucka, no cap. Straight hardbody. He came out here on it, too. He tried fuckin' with that new shit where they projects used to be, but he had to get from down there because niggas wasn't on shit. Hold on."

Squeak chose a fat, nicely rolled Backwood and lit it. She inhaled several times and passed it to Roe. She held the smoke for a bit, then exhaled slowly, haloing the smoke around her head.

She continued, "He came out here to fuck around and saw what I had goin' on. We was doin' a lil' somethin' on the coke side, fuckin' with the weed and shit, not doin' no numbers, but survivin'. All the time Polo was sellin' grams on the heroin and Big Tee was like, 'I'ma drop some of that out here' type shit. I was bored and just happy to be fuckin' with my big cousin like that, so I went along. Soon as he dropped it that shit went haywire. We went from a coupla grams a day to 50-60 grams a day in a week. I guess when he was locked down he made some plans, because the next thing I knew, he was gettin' to the money like crazy. He was wildin' too, knockin' niggas out, puttin' niggas off the set, takin' niggas money and work. When it came to Big Tee there were absolutely no fucks given. He had this shit tight, too."

"If it was so tight, how he get kilt?" Roe asked, as he passed the weed back to Squeak.

Squeak shook her head with a pained expression on her face. For a moment, she didn't speak and avoided Roe's eyes. When she regained her composure, she said, "He got set up by a opp bitch. That shit was crazy! We put a million holes in that bitch and her cousin was the one that did it. Big Tee was fuckin' with a opp bitch the whole time and ain't even know it. He was laid up with the bitch and she text her cuzo that Tee was about to leave. He shoulda had his slammer on him, but his gun was in the car. When Big Tee came out, that bitch ass nigga scored. Kilt my cousin. Bitch ass nigga! Shid, we ain't rest 'til that nigga was in a drawer in the morgue. That bitch died a coupla days later. I miss the fuck out my cuz, cuddy. Tee had us movin' dif'rent. He showed us how to get some money. Had us buyin' these buildings around here instead of a bunch of stupid shit."

"I can see." Roe observed. "This boarded up building trick is like the shit we used to do in the jets. We would leave the boards and shit on the doors and windows of the vacant apartments we would be in. How y'all end up selling heroin though? We ain't never fucked with boy."

"Yeah that's true, Roe, but when Big Tee came to the crib, the city was dry on the coke side. Even the connects he made while y'all was locked up wasn't doin' nothin'. That's when Polo came with the heroin from a connect he met while he was locked up. Tee came out here with that shit, studied the way these niggas out on the Tray sell dope and he set it up perfectly. Next thing we know, bang, we took off. We gettin' to the bag daily, but here come the haters. Big Tee put his hands on a few niggas, offed a few niggas, mafuckas set him up, now he dead. Vanessa, you wanna hit this?"

Vanessa padded over to the dining room and took the Backwood from Squeak. She went back to the kitchen to finish cooking as she smoked.

At the table, Roe poured himself another shot. He held up his glass to Squeak. "To our cousin Terrance, aka Big Tee, aka Terrible. Rest well cuz, we gone live for you and through you."

Squeak touched her glass to his. "Free our big cuddy L.J. and Cuckoo Carl, too. Love you, my nigga Terrible. I'm gone keep my foot on these niggas neck for you."

They both drained their shots.

"Squeak, I gotta come out here and fuck around with you, cuz. It feels good to be around family. At times, I feel like the world just passed us while we was locked up. Shid, I missed my fuckin 20s, my whole fuckin 20s. I'm still trippin' on how our whole entire fuckin' project is gone off the face of the map, like it was never there. I don't even know what to do."

"You don't know what to do?" Squeak asked, as she stood up. She reached into her pocket and pulled out a bankroll wrapped in rubber bands. She tossed the knot of money to Roe. "That's the easiest question you coulda asked me. Get to the money and stay sucka free. First of all, get it in yo' head, this shit ain't the same. These niggas is some new type niggas. I been out here with they ass for years now and half the time I don't understand they way of thinkin'."

Squeak sat back down and Roe tried to hand her the roll of money back.

"Don't insult me, cuddy. Put that shit in yo' pocket," Squeak said, while reaching for another Backwood.

Martell and Pita, left the living room and came over to the dining room table. They both took a seat.

"Where was I?" Squeak asked. "My big cousins showed me how to get money when I was a shorty. Ain't nobody take time to groom the next generations so some of them ain't got a clue. A lot of niggas got took off the street back in the day, same time as us and right after. Them the niggas was sposed to be grooming the next mafuckas. The street rules don't exist no more cuddy, ain't no loyalty. Tell him, Pita, these streets ain't the same as the projects."

Pita was shuffling a deck of cards as he smoked his blunt and listened to Squeak and Roe. "She ain't lyin', big bro. We had a nigga was ridin' with us get mad and run over to the enemies' side because he was a fuck up. Them niggas shot him in the ass and threw him out a second floor window. That nigga healed up and come back to the set like ain't nothin' happen. Some of these lame ass niggas was kickin' it with him, too. Me, Squeak and Lil Fuji slid up on the set and Squeak popped that nigga in both his ass cheeks and told him to get the fuck on."

"I ain't completely sleep on this shit out here," Roe notified them. "It was a lot of dudes comin' to the joint with all this funny ass paperwork showin' where they done gave statements on niggas. We was beatin' they ass, too. Stay the fuck way from 'round me. I ain't gone be fuckin' with niggas like that no way. Just Family. I been tryin' to get a feel for fuckin' with my nephew Bingo, the rest of them little niggas he run with I don't know 'bout them. A few of them seem alright though."

Martell spoke up. "We fuck with Bingo and them, they Family and all, but he do be with some weirdos. Mainly, we bump into them niggas in traffic and shit. We done traded a few hot guns with them too, but that's about it. He was tryna get Terrible to give him some dope, but Tee kept spinnin' the nigga, even though that's our lil' cousin. So I knew something was up with him. I asked Terrible about it and he told me, them niggas don't know how to get money, all they know how to do is get high. He said, they ass will run off with $100 when they could have made $10,000 with you."

"Big Tee ain't wanna fuck with a lot of dudes," Squeak said with a shrug. "Roe, you already know cuddy was super paranoid. They got him the only way they could have and that's with some pussy. Bin is Family though, so I fuck with him. Cuddy owe me a coupla 100 now, but I ain't trippin'. When you holla at him Roe, tell him pick up a phone, ain't no mafucka trippin' on that little bread."

"I'll tell him," Roe said. "I'm gone try and get his mind right."

"Good luck," Squeak said. "Cuddy, it's crazy too that you hoppin' outta Ubers and shit."

"I tried to get Polo to bring me over here, but he said he

wasn't goin' this way," Roe told her. "He was dead serious too, he wasn't goin'."

Pita, Martell and Squeak broke into wild laughter. Roe looked at them quizzically.

"What? What happened? Shid, I wanna laugh too, what happened Squeak?"

When Squeak could finally talk, she said, "Polo came through one day tryna hang and it was real active that day. Opps was slidin' back to back, we was bangin' at they ass. His car got hit a few times, he almost got shot. By the time he left that day, his nerves was bad. That nigga said he ain't never, ever, never for no fuckin' reason coming back on this block."

Pita said, "I thought he would feel like he was home in the projects, but he said hell nall, the projects was safer than this."

"Yeah, he was messin' with my girl Karma from 62nd, he told her to lose his number," Martell said with a snicker.

"I gotta get you out them Ubers, Roe, we almost fired that bitch up," Squeak announced. "I got somethin' for you. You can have one of my low-lows. I got a nice, little Camry you'll prolly like."

"I don't want no hot ass car you been doin' drive-bys in, Squeak."

"Damn cuddy, you think I'd do you like that? Ain't nobody never seen this car. It's damn near new. My man be goin' to the auction and be grabbin' me shit so I can sell. Some shit I keep. I got a coupla cars stashed. Lil Fuji, check it out, Family."

In the living room, Lil Fuji paused the game and came into the dining room area. "'Sup, Freaky?"

"Go get that Camry out the garage, and pull it around front. Park a coupla doors down and don't let nobody see you. Come right back."

"Don't eat up all the chicken," Lil Fuji said.

"Boa, get yo' ass outta here," Squeak said. "You know Vanessa will damn near feed you before she feed me, lil' ass nigga."

Lil Fuji walked to the back door of the apartment, undid the deadbolts and left out the door. Vanessa stopped preparing the meal, walked over to a small basket on the kitchen counter and took a key with an alarm fob out of the basket. She walked over to the back door and held the key out. Seconds later, Lil Fuji opened the door, noticed Vanessa holding the keys for him, took them from her and went back out the door. Vanessa went back to the stove and started fixing two, huge plates of food. When she was done, she sat the plates in front of Squeak and Roe. Pita and the others knew to go in the kitchen and fix their own plates.

Squeak pulled apart a steamy chicken wing. After taking a bite, she said, "Cuddy, if you wanna come out here and get some of this heroin money, I could always use the help. You could make you a nice, five, six month stretch and you'll be good."

"Thanks, Family, but y'all might be too fast for me out this way. I got a few lil' plans and they don't include sellin' heroin and joinin' a full fledged gang war. I think I'ma take it slow, maybe fuck with the weed while I weigh my options. Maybe sell some pills. My man I was locked up with can get me all the exotic weed and designer drugs I want."

"If you got a connect on the pills, I been lookin' for a plug so let me know," Squeak said. "If I can get a steady line on some good hittas, I'll fall all the way back from the heroin trade. I'm surrounded by pill poppin' animals so I know we'll flood the market with some good ass pills. Let me know, cuddy. I'm serious, serious."

"Uh-huh," Roe mumbled as he tucked off into the plate of fried chicken, spinach and corn on the cob. "I got you. This food good as hell, I'm definitely gone have to come out here more often."

Squeak laughed, "Don't hurt yo'self cuddy, there's plenty more in the kitchen. I'll have Vanessa make you a to-go plate, too."

CHAPTER TWENTY-TWO

Across the street from the grammar school they'd once attended, in the park, Polo, Razo and Roe sat on a bench, sharing a bottle of Remy Martin. The grammar school had closed down when their housing development was torn down because now there wasn't a student population. They had tried bussing in kids for a while, but that didn't last long because it was costly and the kids often missed the buses. On a warm, sunny day like today, many ex-residents of the projects gathered at their old park to enjoy the weather and catch up with one another. Plenty of weed was smoked and liquor flowed as loud laughter, cursing and roasting could be heard.

Appearing to be happy that he was home, people walked up to the bench they were occupying to shake Roe's hand or give him a hug.

"It's good to see yo' ass, Roe," Razo said excitedly, as he put his arm around Roe's shoulders. "Family, we ain't never think yo' ass was gone get out."

"Nigga, for a minute there, it felt like I wasn't. How you been though, Family? I been asking Polo 'bout you."

"He told me," Razo replied. "I ain't been doin' shit but workin', nigga. Tryna stay out the way. I got a pretty decent gig, all the overtime I want. Plus, I be workin' my number up in there. That's my spot, I been there since I got out the joint. If you ever need a job let me know, you straight in. All I know is, that gig keeping me from comin' out here in these streets and wrestlin' with these mothafuckas. I don't want no smoke whatsoever with these niggas."

"I ain't ready for a job just yet," Roe said. "I'm tryna get me some shit goin', but I need the bread to get it goin'. I know damn well ain't no fuckin' bank gone loan me the cash, so I got to run it up myself. Plus, I gotta make sure Cuckoo and L.J. straight."

Polo interjected, "Nigga, Cuckoo good, but L.J. super straight. He got some shit going on in the camp he at. That nigga told me don't even send him no money. He said buy him some tobacco and cell phones. He makin' a killin' with that shit. That nigga sent some chick to get the shit from me that I ain't never seen before. Bitch was bad, too."

Razo stood up on the bench and stretched. He said, "Man, L.J. gone get some bread no matter where he at. I miss him and Cuckoo, and Big Tee, them niggas was straight gangstas. My son be out here on some goofy shit. He over there in Englewood. I'm basically just waitin' to get the call that his young ass dead or done got booked for a body or rape or some dumb shit. His mother turned him against me while I was locked up, so I can't tell the young nigga shit. He talkin' 'bout I wasn't there for him. How the fuck was I gone be there for you and I'm in jail, dumb ass nigga? I wish y'all could see these niggas that he lookin' up to out here on this block he claimin'."

Polo's cell phone rang. He answered it. "Waddup, JP? My nigga, what's good? Yeah, it's nice as hell out here. Not really, it's a few bitches, but I ain't seen nothin' for me. That's wassup. Just fuckin' around with Razo and Roe up here at the park. Alright then, fall through. Bring a bottle. Alright, we up here."

When Polo ended his call, Roe asked, "Who the fuck was that?"

"My homie, Joe Perry."

"Who? Do I know this nigga?"

"Nall, he good people though," Polo said.

"You know this nigga, Razo?" asked Roe, turning to Razo.

"N'all," Razo said. "I ain't never know him, only through Polo. I know him enough to just to say wassup. That about it."

Roe turned back to Polo. "So, tell me Polo, just what make this nigga good people? Was y'all locked up together or somethin'?"

"Nall, we wasn't in the system together, but I been fuckin' with the nigga for a minute now, and the nigga ain't never showed nothing but love. You feel me? He the one be gettin' me some good ass numbers on the heroin, and his dope always right. Always a bomb! That nigga can get you whatever you need and more than likely for a good price. He prolly can get you a better price on that weed and them pills."

"I'm straight on my connect, Family. Where this nigga, Joe Perry from?"

"Damn, what's with the questions?" Polo asked. "The nigga from over East."

"Now how you know a nigga from over East that you wasn't locked up with?" Roe asked suspiciously. "Explain that shit to me, just how a nigga from the East side is yo' best friend now? A nigga you ain't meet in the joint at that? Yo' ass be high off that raw coke and just get to meetin' any ole body, friendly ass nigga."

"Yo' paranoid ass," Polo scoffed. "I checked the nigga out. I ain't slow. I had seen the nigga on the gamblin' boat in Indiana a coupla times. One night we was at the blackjack table and the dealer tore our asses up. We chilled and fucked with a few bitches and we got cool."

"You ever went over East with homie?" Razo asked.

"Yeah nigga. I'm tellin' you I fuck with the nigga. He a real one. I been to his crib and everything. Plus, we go skiin' on the regular, the nigga snort coke, too. He don't really hang too tough over East though because them niggas greasy. They be tryna poke niggas. Hold on y'all. What the fuck is goin' on over there?"

Polo stood up and pointed to where a couple of people were leaving the park in a hurry. They hopped in their cars and pulled off. On some of the other benches, different groups of people had begun to get up and walk away.

"I don't know," Razo said. He peered around, trying to identify the threat.

A man hurried past their bench holding the hand of his daughter.

"Aye, homie, why mufuckas movin' around?" Polo asked him.

The man looked back with a worried look on his face. He told them, "Here come a bunch of them young boys from the new houses. They ass got guns and shit. Ain't nobody got time for that goofy shit they be on."

"What they be on, some stickup shit?" Roe asked.

"Nall, not all the time," the man said, with a look on his face like he wanted to go far away. "It's just they some silly lil' niggas. Grown mafuckas don't wanna be around they goofy asses. They into it with niggas and niggas might do a drive-by. The only person gone get hit is somebody that ain't got shit to do with the shit. Here they come. Aye, y'all be smooth, I got my shorty, I'm finta move around."

With his daughter in tow, the man hurried off as the six males ranging in age from their teens to early 20s crossed the street and entered the park. Several of them were obviously carrying weapons and they made no real effort to conceal them. As they swaggered into the bench area, Roe recognized them. He turned to Razo and Polo.

"That's my nephew Bingo and his guys," Roe stated.

"I know a couple of they lil' asses by face, they some fuckin' terrorists," Polo asserted.

Bingo's squad were walking on the benches, just generally being annoying, and one of them kicked over one of the nearly full park garbage cans.

"Bingo! Bingo! Check it out, Family!" Roe called out.

Recognizing his uncle, Bingo came over to the bench and greeted Roe. He nodded his head at Polo, but totally ignored Razo. "Waddup, Unc? I see you and the OGs hangin' tough."

Polo held out the Remy bottle to Bingo. "You want a shot of this here?"

"No thanks, I don't drink that old people ass drink, give me some Cuervo or Patron," Bingo said.

Roe climbed down off the bench. He said, "Fuck all that. Check it out, nephew." He walked to a nearby bench and took a seat. Bingo followed him. "How that shit movin'g for you, nephew?"

Bingo leaned over on one cheek and pulled a bankroll from his back pocket. He handed it to Roe. "I'm through with that shit, Unc. That's for both the weed and them hittas. Make sure you give me some more of those for sure. Them pills was straight hittas! Try to get the same shit if you can."

Roe put the money in his pocket. "I got you. Aye, I went out there and hollered at Squeak ass. She said waddup."

"I gotta go out there with Squeak nem, they ass be on it," Bingo said.

"Nall, stay yo' ass from out there. You don't need to be goin' out there just to try and score some points. Y'all got enough goin' on this way. You need to concentrate on gettin' you some money, nephew."

Bingo held up his hands. "I got you, Unc," he said. "I been tryna get off that savage shit and boss up, but most of the time these opps won't let you. I'm sick of gangbangin' though. Unc, you see I'm bringin' you yo' bread as soon as I get it like you said. How long it gone be before you get at me with some more weed and shit?"

"The shit in my trunk right now," Roe stated as he stood up. "When you finta bounce I'ma pop the trunk and you grab that bookbag. Everything in there."

Bingo stood also and gave Roe a handshake hug. "We gone chill for a minute Unc, then I'm gone grab that out yo' trunk when we 'bout to bounce."

Bingo returned to the bench with his friends and Roe did the same. Some people started to filter back to the bench area of the park, and as soon as they started to feel a little bit more comfortable around the young thugs, two of Bingo's guys began to argue loudly. Their argument escalated into a shoving match in a matter of moments, and that escalated into them pulling guns on one another.

"Look at this shit, Family," Polo said with disgust.

Roe shook his head. At first, Bingo seemed to take it lightly and told them to put away their weapons, but when they didn't obey his orders, he hopped to his feet and began chastising them. He stole on both of them and made them put their guns away and shake hands. They chilled for a while more, but everyone around them on the benches were on high alert now. Sensing that the vibe was gone, Bingo informed them it was time to be out. First he walked back over to Roe's bench.

"Unc, let me grab that and gone get little, these niggas cappin'," he said.

"That ain't cool uppin' no banger on 'yo man," Polo notified him.

"I know old school, that's that nigga Antrell ass, he always startin' shit. He stay clout chasin', he only doin' all that

124

because it's all these people out here. I keep tellin' his ass that shit goofy as hell. He gone up on the wrong nigga and end up on a t-shirt. They wasn't gone shoot shit though, they both was frontin' they move."

Roe took his car keys from his pocket and used the remote to open the trunk of his Camry. "Nephew, I don't give no fuck about none of that shit, just long as they know I take that shit personally. That shit is crazy though, me and Family done got into it plenty of time, but ain't nobody ever upped no pistol on each other. Gone 'head and bust that move and get up outta here before somebody be done called the law."

Bingo walked off and signaled to his guys. They followed him as he walked to the street and went to the trunk of Roe's car. He took the book bag from the trunk and slung it on his back. He closed the trunk lid and they all crossed the street and disappeared into the new homes. Minutes after they were gone, the chill vibe had started to return to the park. Roe, Polo and Razo were reminiscing about the years they looted the stores after the Bulls won the NBA championships when a silver Jeep with the doors missing drove up to the park, and pulled into a parking space. Wearing a Cavaliers Lebron James jersey, a snapback Cleveland Cavs hat, some distressed moto jeans and white Air Force Ones, Joe Perry exited the vehicle, carrying a white bottle of Belair. He walked into the park and made a beeline for Polo when he spotted him.

"Polo, this yo' guy, Joe Perry?" Roe asked.

"Yeah, that's him. Give the nigga a chance, he good people, I'm tellin' y'all."

As Joe Perry neared, Roe looked him up and down. When he reached the bench, his handshake with Polo was hearty, but not so much with Roe and Razo.

With a fake hurt look on his face, Joe Perry said, "Roe, that's how you gone do me? Damn. Long as I been waitin' to meet you."

"What you waitin' to meet me for, homie?" Roe asked with a scowl.

"Damn, my nigga it's all good, you home now," Joe Perry said jokingly. "It's cool though, I know how niggas be when they just come home from them long bits, they don't trust nobody. It's good though, homie. I just know my man Polo been talkin' about you since I met him. This nigga couldn't wait for you to come home. I know you a legend in this shit nigga, and I love to meet new friends. I know when a real nigga come home, he be needin' new friends. I ain't tryna be nothin' but a friend. That's it, that's all."

Roe stood up on the bench and hopped down. He looked Joe Perry directly in his eyes. He said, "Well, Mr. Joe Perry, I'm not in the market for no new friends or nothin' else."

Still not deterred, Joe Perry said, "No harm, no foul my nigga. Like I said, I'm just happy that another real nigga done touched down to these streets. Maybe we'll meet again and have a drink and chop it up like playas."

"That'll never happen, Family," Roe assured him.

"Why you say that?" queried Joe Perry.

Roe reached down and picked the Remy bottle up off the pavement. "Simple," he said. "Because, I'm not a playa, I'm a gangsta. C'mon Razo, let's walk down there and see who on the other end. Look like a coupla bitches down there."

Polo was shocked. "Really Roe? You just gone walk off with the bottle like that? Razo, you up with his bullshit too, hunh?"

Razo smiled as he got down off the bench and followed Roe. Joe Perry looked salty for a moment before he took a seat on the bench and popped open the Belair bottle. He poured Polo a cup and raised the bottle in mock toast to Roe and Razo as they walked across the field to the playground area of the park.

CHAPTER TWENTY-THREE

Roe leaned against the gate at the park, just watching the scenery. His schedule of selling and delivering weed and pills left him with many open gaps in his daily schedule and he often found himself being drawn to the park. He would chop it up with a few of the men and women he knew from the projects when he was hanging, but he didn't consider any of them his friends. Really he was studying them more than anything. The way he heard them talk negatively about people whose faces they smiled in daily, made him really careful about the company he kept. He learned quickly that though the project buildings and row houses were gone, some people had never learned to live any other way. The only reason he managed to notice this was because he'd been away for so long. It amazed him to see how many of them claimed his homeland, but didn't represent it well.

There had always been plenty of hate in the projects, so he was used to that. At first Roe couldn't figure out why some of their actions bothered him so much. It took him awhile to realize it was because there was no balance. Back in the project days, there was plenty of hate, but there was plenty of love, too; much more love. The way it felt so cold at times made him think back to the days when people genuinely cared about one another. The spirit that made them a community just wasn't there anymore. Project people used to look out for one another because they felt like all they had was each other. There was always somebody cooking that would offer a plate, or babysit, or ride here or there, asking if you wanted something back from the store, willing to braid your hair, or walk your child to school. Nowadays, it felt like every man was out for him or herself. They claimed they were from the housing development he'd been born and raised in, but Roe didn't see the connection.

He was broken out of his reverie, by the approach of a man named Gizmo. Gizmo was from the King Houses too, but he was five or six years younger. He knew of their deeds, though he had grown up on the other side of the grammar school, basically a no man's land because of the CHA police station. When he first met him, Roe didn't dislike the man, but now that attitude had changed because of his incessant whining. All the man talked about was what he didn't have and what people weren't giving him. The more Roe thought about it, the more he realized Gizmo was like so many of the guys out here calling themselves street niggas and hustlers. Roe knew many of them looked at him as an out-of-touch hustler that it would be easy to finesse out of work, but they had no idea just how in touch he actually was. Bingo was doing well, except for getting caught with a pistol, he had been going steady and had started selling a couple of pounds a day in weight to customers. Even with the new pistol case, once he made bail, Bingo got right back to the money. Outside of Bingo and Squeak, and a few more good customers, Roe was definitely disappointed in the mentality of the hustlers these days.

Every day on the outside reminded him of the talks he used to have with Posey in the joint. It was crazy because niggas he barely knew were asking him to put them on. They all acted like he was there to single handedly save the drug game by passing out weed, coke, heroin and pills like some sort of savior. He couldn't recall ever receiving any money, visits or mail from a single one of them during the time he was away.

"Roe dog, what up my nigga," Gizmo said. He reached out his hand for a handshake, and Roe halfheartedly shook his hand. "What's happening with you, Family?"

"Shit," Roe said.

"Man, it's dry out here, bro. Ain't nobody out here with no weed or shit. They got the park looking real weak. Non hustlin' ass niggas. Roe, these niggas don't move shit like y'all used to back in the days. I'm tellin' you, you should set this shit up and we can make this shit roll again."

"Nigga, what is you talkin' about?" Roe asked disdainfully. "I ain't settin' shit up. I ain't got nothin' for no nigga to do nothin' with, homie."

"We know you got it, Family," Gizmo said. "When y'all went down, y'all had millions. You niggas still got it. Put the hood on, do it for the streets, Family."

Roe started to snap on Gizmo, but before he could get too worked up, he decided it would be a waste of energy. In a tired voice, he said, "Man, I ain't got no millions. If I did, you think I would be here in the park, sellin' some fuckin' zips of weed to niggas. Now you can gone with all the finessin', what you want?"

"Well, you know I be buyin' a ounce, but I just had to pay my phone bill and the light bill at Granny crib. So I'ma just grab a seven from you, unless you gone front me the whole ounce and let me owe you."

Looking at him like he lost his mind, Roe said, "Look man, ounces cost $200. Ain't no sevens or shit else. Ain't no fronts, layaways or whatever. When you got $200, hit me up or call Bingo. Better yet when you get your money, call Bingo from now on."

Roe pushed himself away from the gate and walked away. As he did, Gizmo called out to him, "That's wassup, Roe. You know you my nigga! I got you on that. I'm gone get at you with that bread. Aw-ight my dude. Check you later."

All Roe could do was shake his head. He continued across the park until he was near the basketball courts. He was standing near the basketball rims watching some guys play a three on three game, when a woman's voice called his name in a long and irritating manner.

"Rrrrooooooeeeeee. Rrrrooooooooee."

He turned to see who was calling him with a smile on his face, but that smile quickly melted when he saw it was Felicia.

"Oh hey, Fefe," he said dryly.

"A bitch can't get no hug?" she asked.

As she came toward him with her arms widespread, he took a quick inventory of her looks. Inwardly he admitted, time had not been good to her. Her shapely body was long gone, and someone left a bloated, stretch mark covered, bag of cellulite in its place. She was currently stuffed in a cheap, multi-colored dress from Rainbow that didn't leave much to the imagination. Her face was swollen from alcohol and scarred from years of fights with her own man, and from fighting other women over theirs. Though he really didn't want to, Roe returned her embrace when she hugged him. She hugged him way too long and he was forced to extract himself, gently but firmly.

"Boy, yo' ass smell good, that shit done made my pussy wet," Felicia purred, putting her hand on his chest. "Damn, they said you look good and I see they wasn't lying for once."

"They wasn't lying about you neither," Roe murmured, removing her hand from his chest.

"Humph, I hope you ain't listenin' to no haters. These bitches is just mad because they can't be me. Goofass broads. They got me fucked up. When I find the bitch that keep sayin' I got bed bugs, I'm gone whup her ass, too. Air mattress havin' hoes, whole house came from Rent-a-Center. They got me fucked up for real. But fuck all that, I'm just glad we finally linked, now I can get some of that just-came-home dick. What's up though Family?"

"Ain't shit up, Fefe."

"Boy, stop actin' like that. You know I miss you. I was in love with you when they locked you up."

Roe laughed. "I couldn't tell. You ain't visit me not one time. Never sent me a letter, and not a damn dime of the money I left with you. That's a fucked up kinda love."

"You ain't even got to be tryna judge me. Shit wasn't all good when you was gone, niggas beat on me, some of yo' other bitches jumped on me and tried to mess up my face. Shit wasn't all good. You know what..."

Felicia turned and hid her face like she was crying.

Roe laughed even harder this time. "I done seen it all now. I finally got to see a real life crocodile cry."

Felicia took her hands from her dry face and turned to Roe. She said, "Fuck you, Roe, I was about to cry! You hurt my fuckin' feelings. I'm sick of niggas like you pissin' on me and tellin' me it's rainin'. You got me fucked up."

"Girl, what the fuck is you talkin' about?"

"Alright, I'm just gone put it out there. I need some help and I thought because we used to be in love, for old times' sake you would help a bitch out."

Roe started laughing hysterically, but he stopped when he saw the look on her face. "Felicia, you serious ain't you?"

"Yeah, I'm serious, I'm in a jam and I thought maybe a nigga that loved me, maybe would help me." To add emphasis to her conning, she sniffled and forced a tear from her eye. "I guess you was just fuckin' me like everybody else and really didn't love me."

"Girl, you is tweakin'! You do remember you used to steal money from me, you done fucked Family members of mine, and I ain't heard from you in years? Hold on, hold on, hold on though. As if it really makes a difference, what is it that you could possibly need help with that would make you ask me? Is it another abortion? I already paid for two of those and I doubt if they were even mine, but so what. What is it that you need?"

Fefe's alcohol soaked brain allowed her to mistake his sarcasm for sincerity. She rushed forward and hugged him, though this time he didn't return the hug. She gushed, "I knew my baby Roe still loved me. Fefe sorry if she was bad while you was gone, but you was gone for so long and I was so lonely. But that's all over now. I knew you was gone come back to Big Fe. You want yo' dick sucked don't you?"

"Not right now, let me know what you need, Fefe?" Roe asked with an earnest look on his face, after he broke her embrace.

"It ain't a lot, but my son that's 18 done got into it with these niggas over here in Englewood on some of that goofy block shit. He shot two of them niggas, and got locked up. He got a high bond and he need a lawyer. I need my king out here with his family. Them muthafuckas from the block is threatenin' my other kids and shit."

Roe put his hand on his chin like he was thinking. "How much is his bond?"

"He only need 15 bands to walk. I know you rich so that ain't nothin' to you. The lawyer I talked to said he'll represent him for $20,000, so I can give him the bond slip. You can wait a while before you give me the rest. What you think baby?"

Roe pretended to give it some thought, until he could no

longer keep a straight face. He burst out laughing. "I think that's the stupidest, craziest shit I ever heard and you have to be one sick ass bitch to even open yo' mouth and say some bullshit like that to me."

Shocked, Fefe opened and closed her mouth several times in disbelief. "Why is you even sayin' that Roe?" she whined. "Don't be like that. We'll be back together if you do this. You can even move in with me."

Roe roared with laughter. "You is even crazier than I thought, Felicia. No thanks to moving in yo' piece of shit apartment with yo' gangbangin' ass sons, bedbugs and yo' THOTin' ass daughters. You asked me to move in with you? I would rather spend the rest of my life in the joint. Bitch, you is crazy. Matter of fact, here."

Roe pulled a bankroll from his pocket. He thumbed through it until he found a $20, which he tossed on the ground. "Fuck you and yo' son. I hope he rot in jail, like you left me to do. That $20 is all I got on his bail and lawyer. You can spend it on you a drank, a gallon of bleach to drink or some vinegar to douche that tired cat and then maybe you can sell $20,000 worth of pussy. Might take you 20 years, but that's okay, because that's right around the time, yo' bitch ass son will be gettin' out of jail. That's even if he wants to leave after spending 20 years of suckin' niggas' dicks and gettin' fucked. Bitch, I actually gave you more money than you're worth."

"That's how you feel, Roe? Really? Fuck you! You ain't shit, that's why you ass gone end up back in the penitentiary, jailbird ass nigga! You just mad 'cause I won't give you this pussy! You ain't shit! All these bitch ass niggas round here actin' like you god, you ain't shit! Motherfuck you, when my son get out, I'm gone have him pop yo' bitch ass!"

Instead of getting angry, Roe walked to his car as FeFe rained insults on his ears. He looked back and saw her scoop the $20 and stick it into her cleavage. Satisfied with the fact that she'd picked it up, he kept walking. He got in his car, started it and drove away; he'd had his fill of the park for the day.

CHAPTER TWENTY-FOUR

It was raining cats and dogs as Roe dashed from the hallway of his aunt Martha's building to his car. The raindrops were of the large, cold sort and made Roe shiver a bit as he slid into his Camry. He tossed his book bag on the back seat and started the car, turning on the defroster as he warmed the car for a few moments. When he drove away, as was his normal routine, he filled most of his weed orders in the morning. On his way to get his morning cup of coffee, he spotted a familiar face on the bus stop. He pulled out of traffic and honked his horn several times, but his friend didn't recognize it was him.

Roe put the car in reverse and backed up to the bus stop, letting the window down. "Razo! Razo! Where you goin', Family?"

Razo leaned down and looked in the car. "Waddup, Family? I'm on my way to work."

"Fuck you doin' on the bus?"

"Trans went out in my truck," Razo replied.

"Get in boy, I'ma spin you to work."

"You sure? My shit over by Cicero."

"Get yo' ass in, nigga."

Razo climbed in and Roe pulled off after they shook hands.

"Good to see you, my nigga," Razo said cheerily. "Thanks for the ride too, Family. I'm tryna get my truck back on the road before the winter, but I gotta see. Shit been tight around the crib with the new baby, and my sister kids stayin' with us. Damn, nigga it been like a month since that day we was at the park."

"What day?" Roe asked, stopping at a stop light.

"That day when yo' nephew nem had mafuckas running out the park for shit. When Polo tried to introduce you to his corny ass homie."

"Okay, okay. Damn, that's been a month?"

"Yeah. What you been doin'?"

"Doin' my little shit, tryna figure shit out. Things ain't been bad, well with the exception of my nephew gettin' locked up. Bingo done got caught with two more bangers after he was already out on bond for another pistol case. He was doin' good, too. Remember the shorty that pulled the pistol at the park that day? His name Antrell, he been handlin' Bingo's operation while he locked up, but I ain't heard from shorty in a coupla days."

"What that nigga Polo been on?" Razo inquired.

"You know that nigga, all he wanna do is get drunk, gamble and snort coke. I ain't mad at him, but I ain't on none of that. I love the nigga, but I feel like I can't trust his decision-makin' at times. Not like back in the days. I get it though. Doin' all that time, L.J. still gone, Cuckoo doing natural life and Big Tee gettin' killed took a lot out of all of us, but we still gotta live. The Houses gone, everybody we fucked with either moved, dead or ain't on shit. That shit have me feelin' lost as hell some days."

Razo shifted uncomfortably in the passenger seat. He said, "You prolly gone think I'm bullshittin', but you sound like you depressed, Family. I know I was when I came home. Shid, you niggas raised me, and y'all wasn't there no more. Wasn't no real game to come home to, and that was prolly good because I ain't been locked back up. I fuck with Polo, but you know he was always an intense ass nigga, 'specially when he snortin' yay all the time. My nigga, you might wanna talk to a mafucka, I mean I ain't go to no psychiatrist or shit, but I can't lie, talkin' to my wife and being around her helped me out a lot, Family."

"Family, I can't talk to none of these bitches," Roe said. "All they ass want is some money. A lot of they ass think I'm rich, either that or I'm just the fresh outta jail dick. I mean I been fuckin' like crazy, but I can't trust none of these bitches, they all the same. I'm gettin' tired of that shit already. Never thought I would see the day, I was tired of gettin' pussy."

Razo nodded in agreement. "I never thought I would see the day that I agree with yo' ass. Well, Family all women ain't bitches, and all bitches ain't women. One thing my wife told me that helped me was, you gotta grow the fuck up. You can't hold onto all that old shit. I mean the principles and shit yeah, but the rest of that shit you gotta let go. We damn near dinosaurs, Family. We 'bout to be extinct, bro. The reason why a lot of niggas be fucked up when they come home is because they can't change. You gotta be able to change, we ain't kids no more." Razo pointed to a building. "That's my gig right there. Pull up on the left, next to the office door."

Roe followed his instructions, steering the car into the parking lot. He asked, "You really like workin', bro?"

Razo thought about it. He replied, "Yeah. Yeah, I do. The money ain't as good as some of the money we saw, but it takes care of my family. I can't complain because we was working for 15 cent an hour in the joint. In the streets, all the money we made came with a heavy price. At work, I ain't gotta worry 'bout the stickup man, the cops, the guys, the feds or none of that. Like they say, you can't put a price on peace of mind. I'm 'bout to get out of here, so I can clock in early. Plenty much love, Roe. I appreciate the ride. Be smooth, Family."

Razo got out of the car and walked around it, as he headed for the office entrance Roe rolled down the window and said, "Razo, check it out for you go in there, Family."

"Yeah?" Razo said as he walked back to the car.

Roe looked up at his friend. "Razo, don't worry 'bout the truck, I got you. When you get off work give me call. I'm gone give you this car."

"What? Stop playin', Roe."

"You know I don't play like that. I'm dead ass. I'll bring you the title and keys when you get off work. Squeak showed me some love when I wasn't driving, now I'm just passin' it on to one of my Family members. Hit my line when you get off."

The two men shook hands and Roe drove away, leaving Razo standing in the rain shaking his head as he stared after the car. Roe stopped and got a cup of coffee and a donut and slowly drove back to King's Place, the new housing development. The rain had stopped, but it was still chilly and the park was empty. He decided to blow off some steam by going to the gym and getting a workout in. As he cruised the blocks headed for the new gym, he spotted Antrell standing on a corner, one street over. He swung the block and pulled up on Antrell. The boy was startled to see Roe and he kept his hands in his pants like he had a gun.

Roe let the window down. "Little homie, what's good with it?"

"Shit. I ain't on shit. What you on?" Antrell asked nervously as he looked around.

"It's goodie," Roe replied. "Tryna see what's up with you and that few lil' dollars. Is you done? You shoulda been ready for some more."

"They say they don't like that so it's taking longer." Antrell said, obviously lying. "Then Little Buddy got stuck up for a lot of three-fives."

"Yeah? That's the first I'm hearin' of all this. Why you ain't been let me know?"

Avoiding Roe's eyes, Antrell said, "I tried callin' you a couple of times, but yo' phone was goin' straight to voicemail, so I sent you a text, you ain't get it?"

"Nope, I ain't see no missed calls or no texts. But fuck all that, how much money do you got?"

"I don't know," Antrell said with a shrug. "I got to go count it, I know you busy so soon as I count it, I'ma call you, so answer yo' phone."

"I ain't doin' nothin', I'll wait," Roe insisted.

"Uhhh, I can't get in the crib right now, my granny left out," Antrell explained. He looked down the block behind Roe's car. "Aye, big bro, here come the security officers. They be on bullshit with me, tryna write up my granny. I'ma call you."

Before Roe could react, Antrell dipped between the two buildings directly behind him and disappeared. The King's Place security force car drove by slowly and the guards inside the car mean-mugged Roe, but kept driving along. Roe pulled off and drove around the corner, circling the blocks looking for Antrell, to no avail—he was long gone. Roe pulled over and parked. He called Antrell's number several times. On the fourth try, Antrell answered.

"Where you went, lil' homie? Them people wadn't on nothing."

"First of all, old head, I ain't yo' homie," Antrell said with much more confidence than he'd just shown a few moments ago. "Damn, yo' old ass slow as hell. How you don't know you been stained? Ain't no money, nigga, I ain't Bingo! You can't make all the money and my ass don't have nothin'. Fuck that. That shit gone. We got robbed. Tell yo'self whateva you gotta tell yourself to make this easier to swallow."

"So, you sayin' you took that?" Roe asked calmly.

"If that's what you need to hear, old ass nigga, then yeah, I took that. The only reason I ain't gone take no more from you is because you Bingo's people. Take that loss nigga because really it's yo' fault."

"How is it my fault that you're takin' something from me, if you don't mind me askin'?" Roe asked sarcastically. "You have got to explain this to me."

Not catching the sarcasm in Roe's voice, Antrell answered, "This is on you because you came out of jail thinkin' you was still that nigga. You ain't been that nigga in years, my dude. The fuck? You a used-to-be my nigga. Don't nobody give a fuck about that old shit you did in a place that don't even exist no more. Now like I said, take the loss and get over it. Please don't try to flex so I don't have to air yo' old ass out."

Roe got hot under the collar at being threatened. "What you say lil' nigga?" he roared into his cell phone.

"You heard me, OG, don't get that Toyota fired up. Now get off my line."

The line went dead and Roe could only stare at his phone in disbelief. He made another call. "Polo, where you at?"

"Where you need me to be?"

"How soon can you meet me at the cleaners?" Roe asked.

"On my way, be there in ten minutes."

····

Roe parked on the street in front of the dry cleaners. Polo pulled up behind him minutes later and parked. Roe hopped out of his car and walked to Polo's car.

"Polo, you won't believe this shit," Roe started, seconds before he noticed Joe Perry smiling at him from the passenger's seat of Polo's Audi A8 and clammed up. He nodded to Joe Perry and stepped back from the car door as he said, "Check it out, Polo."

Polo moved to get out of the car and Joe Perry put his hand on his door handle, also. Polo looked over at him. "Yo, JP hold fast, let me holla at this nigga real quick. I'll be right back, foolie."

"You sure, bro?" Joe Perry asked, his voice pregnant with concern. "Lil' bro looks stressed out, he might need both of our help. I can probably help, too."

Impatiently, Polo raised his hand. He raised his voice a bit when he said, "He good, man. Let me holla at him. If it's somethin' I need your help on, I'll let you know."

Joe Perry released the door handle and sat back in the seat. "Ok, smooth, my nigga. You g'one 'head. Just let me know if I can do anything. Roe needs to know I got his back too if he ever needs anything."

"Yeah, I'll tell him that," Polo said as he got out of the car. He walked over to Roe. Joe Perry watched through the window as Roe put his arm around Polo's shoulders and walked him to the middle of the block. There they proceeded to have what appeared to be a very animated conversation. Minutes later Roe went to his car and Polo walked back to his car and got in. After Roe pulled off, Polo pulled away behind him, though he turned in the opposite direction.

"So what's up with Roe, he good?" Joe Perry asked.

"He Gucci. It wasn't nothin'."

"You sure? It didn't look like he was okay. I mean if I can help in any way let me know."

"It wasn't no big deal," Polo replied. "Young nigga just having bitch problems. Aye though, I'm 'bout to drop you at yo' truck. I forgot I gotta go do somethin'."

"I'll slide with you," Joe Perry offered.

"Nall, I'm good, I'll get up with you later."

CHAPTER TWENTY-FIVE

Antrell and his friend Rio sat on the bed in the bedroom Antrell lived in at his grandmother's apartment in King's Place Apartments. They were both scrolling through social media sites on their cell phones and smoking weed.

"So, why you ain't just gone give that man his paper, bro?" Rio asked without looking up from his phone.

"Fuck him. On God, I ain't givin' that nigga shit," Antrell replied. "He ain't gone do shit. I needed that. I was just tryna wait 'til the nigga gave me like ten pounds, but his bitch ass ain't never do it."

"I don't know about this," Rio said warily. "Bingo told me them niggas was killers and shit. They used to run the projects that was here first. Plus, that's Bingo uncle, he a good nigga, bro. On bro nem, he fuckin' with us, makin' sure we get some money. That shit ain't right. Roe a real one. Facts."

Antrell passed Rio the weed. When Rio accepted it, he laughed. "Yo' soft ass shole ain't got no problem smokin' his weed. All that shit don't even matter, though. Where Bingo at now, nigga? That's my A1 from day one, but he in that place, while we out here tryna make a way. Bingo gone have to understand and if he don't, fuck him too."

Rio exhaled weed smoke. "Besides that, Trell, you gettin' into it with niggas and ain't even got no guns. All we got is that raggedy ass .380 with two bullets in it. You traded our fucking .40 for some damn lean."

"Shid, I needed that lean, my fuckin' stomach was hurtin' and I needed to pour up. You worried about the wrong shit, Rio. I'm gone sell a coupla ounces and buy a heater. The rest of that shit, I'm smokin' and sellin'. My birthday next week and I'm gone be litty. While you talkin', we had guns, but you niggas kept gettin' caught with them and shit. Bingo done got caught with three, you just threw one and Kev got caught with one, now his dumb ass on house arrest."

"I'm just saying nigga, if you run off with that, once that's gone what we got?" Rio asked, trying to appeal to his friend's common sense. "You seem to forget that wasn't nobody fuckin' with us through here before the OG gave Bingo that shit. Plus, he made sure we was all eatin', bro. He put us on some bread and now you wanna take the man's shit."

Antrell looked up from his phone at Rio. "You sound like a real bitch right now, boi. On my Granny we ain't need that old ass nigga. We was gone eat anyway. Man, mothafuck Roe! What he gone do? Ride up and talk some of that old ass gangsta shit? That shit don't move me. It was two pounds, that nigga better chalk that shit up and get on with his life. We pumped that shit up with Bingo, so that nigga owed us. I'm just takin' what's mine really."

Rio leaned over to pass Antrell the weed, but he waved the duck off and picked up a pack of Backwoods cigars. He opened the pack and inspected several cigars, but they were all broken. He tossed the pack on the floor.

"Damn, we gotta hit the gas station," Antrell announced.

There was a knock at the apartment door just then.

"Get that for me, Rio," Antrell said. "I'm tryna find my other Tim."

Rio got off the bed and left out of the bedroom to answer the door. At the door he asked, "Who that?"

"This is Stanley from downstairs," the knocker said.

"Who?"

"Stanley. I live on the first floor, Tawanda's husband. You guys have a package from Amazon. The guy left it in the hallway. Someone might take it so I thought I'd bring it up for you guys. Neighborly duty and all."

Rio unlocked the door and opened it, and a masked gunman immediately pushed him backwards into the apartment. While the first gunman secured Rio, a second gunman oozed in behind him and closed the apartment door. He looked at Rio and shook his head.

"That's not him," the second gunman told the first one in hushed tones. He pointed his gun at Rio's head. He said, "One chance nigga, where's he at? Don't talk, point."

Rio pointed in the direction of Antrell's bedroom. The second gunman went in that direction. As he rounded the doorframe, Antrell was just coming from under his bed with the black Timberland boot he'd been looking for. As he got to his knees, he only had time to register that there was someone else in the room, before the gunman smacked him senseless with his pistol. Holding his face in horror, he looked up at the gunman as he pulled his mask off.

"Now what was all that tough ass shit you was saying on the phone?" Roe asked menacingly. "And where the fuck is my money?"

Antrell cowered on the floor, holding the boot over his head. "I was just fuckin' with you. On my baby, I was gone bring you that."

Polo marched Rio into the room and deposited him on the floor beside Antrell. He asked, "This the tough one was talkin' all the shit on the phone 'bout what he was gone do?"

"Hell yeah, this him. I wish you coulda heard his bitch ass talkin' all that shit. I was old nigga this, and old head that. Said he was gone air my car out and a whole bunch other slick ass shit he was sayin'."

Without warning, Polo whacked Antrell across the head with his pistol. Antrell howled as he fell. He grabbed his head and rolled around the floor in pain.

"Shut yo' ass up makin' all that noise, bitch!" Roe hissed. "Get yo' ass up!"

As he got to his knees, Antrell whined, "I'm sorry, I was just talkin' shit, I was high. I was gone bring yo' money to you."

"Fuck all that now, nigga," Roe said angrily. "Where the mufuckin' money at? Turn them pockets out, bitch!"

Rio started to turn out his pockets, but Roe pushed him out the way. He held his gun to Antrell's head as he turned out his pockets and handed it to Roe. Roe checked the money quickly.

"Nall, nigga, this ain't all, where the rest of it?"

"That's all I got," swore Antrell. "I still got some weed, like a pound and a half."

"Where it's at, nigga?" Roe asked. "And where Bingo's work phone, too?"

"The phone on the bed and the weed in that blue tote by the bed," Antrell offered fearfully.

While Roe got the phone and the weed, Polo leaned against the door jamb and kept watch on both boys. Once he got both items, he nodded his head at Polo and he came over and stood over the boys with him. Roe pointed his gun at Antrell's head and Polo pointed his at Rio.

"Sorry lil' homie, you was in the wrong place at the wrong time," Roe said to Rio. "I actually like you, but this big mouth, fake gangsta ass nigga gotta go, and I can't leave you around to tell on me."

Both boys realized they were about to die and Antrell fell to pieces. Rio was a bit more controlled than him, but just barely as tears rolled down his cheeks.

Antrell scooted closer to Roe, begging, "I'm sorry, I'm sorry! I swear I was just playin'. I was gone finish sellin' everything and give you the money! Please! Please! Please don't kill me!"

Polo put his gun to Rio's head and prepared to pull the trigger. Rio's shoulders sagged as he closed his eyes and prepared to die.

"Please don't kill my grandson and his friend in my house," Antrell's grandmother said. She was standing in the doorway of the bedroom behind them, wearing a housecoat and slippers.

Startled, Polo and Roe whirled around and aimed their guns at her, but she walked forward into the room in spite of their weapons. She pulled some money from her housecoat pocket and offered it to Roe.

"Please don't kill them," she repeated. "I don't have much money, what I have is all there. You can come back on the 3rd of every month when I get my pension, and I'll give you some money until his debt is paid. Just don't kill him, I know he's a stupid boy, but he can't help it, his daddy was stupid too."

Roe hesitated to take the money, but Polo snatched it. Polo tucked the money in his pocket and retrained his gun on Rio. He looked at Roe, waiting for the go sign.

"I can't let him live after this, and now you done came in

here and seen us," Roe said.

The elderly lady put her withered old hand on Roe's arm. She said, "I ain't seen nothin', baby. I coulda called the police and I didn't. I grew up in the Martin Luther King Houses too, and I know how to be quiet and don't concern myself about things that ain't my business. Antrell ain't a bad boy, he just stupid. His daddy is dumb too, so it ain't his fault. I'ma put him out after today though. His momma moved to San Antonio with her job and he ain't want to leave so he could finish school, but he ain't been goin' to school. Young man, I promise you, he gone be on the next thing smokin' to San Antone, if you let him live. Lord Jesus is my witness, you won't see him again. He can't even come back to visit me after this."

Roe looked at Polo questioningly, who shrugged his shoulders. Polo said, "It's up to you, but now it's a triple homi. This lady ain't did shit neither, but have a dumb ass grandson."

Roe turned back to Antrell, he put the gun to his head and bit his lip. Instead of shooting him, he muffed him to the floor. To Antrell, he said, "I want to do you so bad, I can taste it. Yo' granny just saved yo' worthless life boy, you better get yo' ass outta town like she said, because if I see you in the streets, she can't save you." He picked up the weed and handed it to Rio with the trap phone. He pointed at Antrell, though he was talking to Rio when, he said, "Stay away from him and niggas like him. He almost got you killed. Like I told you, it wasn't personal, I think you're a good dude, so I'm gone give you a chance. Finish that up and then we'll talk numbers. Now get outta here."

Clutching the weed and cell phone, Rio jumped to his feet and never looked back as he made his exit.

Before Roe and Polo exited, Roe said, "Boy, don't think this a joke. Next time ain't no talkin' at all, and you ain't gone see me comin'. Sorry about disrespectin' your house, ma'am, but we had to address this matter."

They walked to the door and Roe stopped and looked at Polo for a moment. Rolling his eyes, Polo dug in his pocket and tossed the money he took from the old lady back at her feet.

"That's his busfare," Roe said. They turned and left the apartment.

CHAPTER TWENTY-SIX

Roe walked into the coffee shop to get his morning cup of coffee. He walked past his friend, Bone, an older guy wearing a newsboy hat on top of his long, grey dreadlocks, sitting at a window table. He was reading a newspaper with a chess board set up in front of him. Roe nodded at him and Bone tipped his head.

Roe waited his turn to order and once he made it to the counter, he ordered, "Medium with four sugars and four creams. Banana nut muffin, too." Without looking over his shoulder, he asked, "What you want?"

"Small with three creams, and one of them jelly donuts," Bone said.

"You got that?" Roe asked the server.

The employee nodded as he went to complete the order. When he returned with the coffee and baked goods, Roe paid for everything and carried it over to the table. He took a seat across from Bone.

"You know it cost to sit in that chair, young God," Bone remarked, looking over his reading glasses at Roe.

"Maybe it will, maybe it won't, that remains to be seen, sir."

Bone folded his newspaper. "Well, young sir ain't nothing to it, but to do it."

"Say less," Roe responded, moving a piece on the chess board to start a game which Bone won easily.

"You gonna be buying my coffee and donuts for the rest of my life playing like that," Bone observed.

"Let's go again," Roe said, as he began to set the pieces up.

Bone knocked over his king. "I don't want to play you when yo' mind ain't on the game. That's a waste of my time and yours. You wasn't even in that game, God. What's wrong with you?"

Roe looked away. "I can't even front, Bone. I almost feel like I'm lost out here."

"I figured as much," Bone said, stirring his coffee.

"How you know that?"

"Shid, I got eyes, God. I see you riding them streets every day looking for the answers, but they ain't gone magically appear. Sorry, Money-making Monroe, but the world moved on without you when you was gone. Life is funny like that. You gotta move on with it or get left behind."

As if to give Roe time to let that thought sink in, Bone bit his donut and took a sip of his coffee. Roe did the same. For a bit he was content to watch people make their way up and down the sidewalk outside, on their way to work or wherever.

Wistfully, Roe said, "When I was in the joint and people were tellin' me they was tearin' down our home, I didn't really believe it. I definitely didn't know they were destroyin' our way of life. Everything is different. Everything. It feel fucked up to never be able to see the place where you from ever again."

Bone nodded his head. "I get it," he said. "And you may not wanna hear it, but them days ain't never coming back. I know you was a younger God when y'all got locked up, but you lived so fast at an early age, you got caught in a time warp. By that I mean, the past is gone, the present is different and the future is unsure. You got a lot of life to live, God. Don't let the way you used to live keep you trapped in a little box a couple of blocks long. This world is huge."

"You sound like my big homie, Posey. He used to run with my pops in the projects back in the days. He was in the joint with me, in some ways he helped me become a man, now that I think about it."

"Sounds like a source of wisdom, God," Bone commented.

"To tell you the truth, Bone, a lot of the shit I thought I wanted when I got out, I don't want that shit no more. It just ain't the same no more without the guys anyway. I thought we would be able to do the same thing for the rest of our lives, but now that I got out and I see people that been doing the same

145

thing all that time, I don't know no more."

Bone laughed. "What you don't know, God?"

Surprised at his laughter, Roe asked, "What? How is it funny that I don't know what's going on?"

"I'm not laughing at that. I'm laughing because you done fucked around and grew up and don't even know it. Ain't nothing wrong with wanting to do more and see more in life. Believe it or not, I been all over this globe. Amsterdam, Ghana, New York, L.A, Philly, Brazil, just seeing how other people live. And when I came back home, I would be looking at Negroes that ain't moved an inch since I was gone. He lived and loved his life, but that was his life. That was the fatal flaw with a lot of people that lived in the projects, they thought they had to live the way everybody else was living. The way a lot of y'all was living only bought hurt and pain, but you think that you're not being real if you don't live that way. It's okay to do something different Roe, especially if you're dissatisfied with the way you're living. If anything, live for your brothers that aren't here, and for your brothers that ain't leaving them white devils' prisons. Realize you got a second chance and it's up to you what you do with it. And you're still young enough to live your dreams out, you just gotta figure out what you wanna do with your life."

Roe stood up and picked up his coffee cup. He tipped over his king on the chess board. "As much as it would pleasure me to sit here and kick yo' butt around this board for the remainder of the morning, I gotta make a run. Thanks for the chess game and the life game, Bone. Tomorrow?'

Bone sat back. "Unless the Creator has a different opinion, I'll be right here waiting on my next victim. Matter of fact, he just walked through the door. Peace God."

"Peace," Roe said. He left the store and got in his car.

CHAPTER TWENTY-SEVEN

At the corner of 43rd and King Drive, two beautiful women crossed the street in front of the car ahead of Roe's Mazda SUV. Both women wore business suits with sensible heels and were carrying food bags and soft drink cups in their hands. The taller of the two women, was light-skinned and appeared to be older than her companion, who was shorter by several inches. The shorter, younger woman had cinnamon colored skin and dreadlocks that were swept up into an intricate braided halo. They were talking as they walked, and the taller woman must have said something amusing, because the other woman smiled a ravishing smile that instantly captivated Roe.

All Roe could do was stare at her with his mouth open. She must have felt the intensity of his gaze because she looked directly at him. She locked eyes with him for a few seconds, before giving him a shy smile and continuing across the street. The intersection light turned green and though he didn't want to proceed, several cars behind him honked. He tried to let the cars to the right of him go ahead so he could pull out of traffic, but they wouldn't stop honking behind him. He drove through the intersection slowly, all the while looking over his shoulder at the women. He saw them go into a storefront office there.

As soon as he saw enough space to jump over a lane, he cut the car off on his right and pulled to the curb. Hurriedly, he exited the vehicle and scampered through traffic, having several near misses with oncoming cars. As he got to the sidewalk in front of the store front, he looked up at the large sign, it read Community Development Inc. He stepped back and looked at the other store fronts, but he was absolutely sure she'd come inside the one in front of him. Throwing caution to the winds, he pulled the glass door open of the Community Development office and stepped inside.

The receptionist at the front desk of the office, a young, Black male sporting a yellow dress shirt with a navy blue bowtie was eating lunch, but looked up at Roe. "May I help you, sir?" he asked, wiping his mouth with a napkin. "Do you have an appointment?"

Roe looked around at the offices as he placed his hands on the receptionist desk. "Nall, I ain't got no appointment. I'm just looking for a lady that came in here."

"What you mean you're looking for a lady that came in here?" asked the receptionist with his face registering alarm. "Turner! Turner!"

"Whoa, whoa, whoa, playboy not like that."

A tall, baldhead, brown skinned man wearing a beard strode from one of the rear offices. His fitted sweater and slacks showed he had a muscular physique. His gaze was fixed on Roe, as he asked in a deep baritone, "Torry, what's goin' on man?"

The receptionist answered, "This guy just came through the door saying that he's looking for a lady that came in here."

"Okay, well calm down, there's no need to panic," Turner said without taking his eyes off of Roe. He offered Roe his hand. "I'm sure there's a good reason. How you doin', brother?"

Roe shook his hand. "I'm good. Yo' name is Turner?"

"Yeah."

"You used to work at the fieldhouse in the King's Houses?"

"For many years. Did you used to live there?"

"Yeah," Roe said. "You don't remember me? I'm Roe, I mean Monroe, I played field hockey for you that year we almost won the Park District Championship. When they was cheating for them white boys from Bridgeport."

Turner stepped back and looked Roe up and down for a moment, then grabbed him up in a huge embrace. When he released Roe, he said, "Of course I remember you, Monroe! You was a bad, lil' joker, but you ain't never give up. You came home a while ago then?"

"Nall, I was sposed to been came home, but I was down there wildin' out," Roe confessed. "I'm good now, though. Been home for close to a year now."

Turner pulled Roe over to a small table in the lobby and they both took a seat. He adjusted his slacks before crossing his legs and looking at Roe earnestly. "So, you didn't know I was here, did you meet one of the women co-workers and had an appointment?"

"Not really," Roe said sheepishly. "You probably gone think I'm tweakin', but I was sitting at the light right here and I saw an angel walk into this office. I didn't even know what y'all did up in here, but I just had to meet her. She so bad, I mean beautiful, Turner, her smile, her eyes. Damn!"

Turner laughed. "Well, I'm quite sure though my wife is beautiful, you're aren't talking about her. The woman with the beautiful smile and eyes is our mentee, Tamara. They were just bringing me and Torry there some lunch." He leaned forward to stage-whisper, "She's in my office, and she can hear you. Don't worry about it though, she's good people, I'll introduce you. C'mon."

Roe followed Turner into his spacious office. There Turner introduced him to both his wife and Tamara. When Roe shook Tamara's hand there was a small spark. He couldn't let her hand go as he lost himself in the prettiest brown eyes he'd ever seen in his life. Up close, her smile was even more warm and radiant. Her brown skin had a soft glow to it and he could smell a honey citrus scent coming from her locs. Turner and his wife were saying something, but Roe couldn't hear them for the blood pounding in his ears. Tamara seemed to be just as lost in his gaze as he was in hers, nor did she try to take back her hand from him.

With a smile on his face, Turner came forward and touched them both on the shoulder, breaking the spell. "Monroe, I'm about to walk the ladies to their cars, but don't go anywhere. I want to holla at you real quick about that investment you wanted to know about."

"Oh yeah, the investment," Roe said awkwardly, releasing Tamara's hand. "My bad, Tamara got me stuck looking in her pretty eyes."

Tamara blushed a bit, as she shouldered her purse. Before leaving the office, she said, "Turner, I left some of my business cards with you just in case someone needs my contact information. It was nice to meet you, Monroe. I hope to see you around."

Roe waved as they left, taking a seat in front of Turner's desk. Turner returned shortly, took his seat behind his desk, and opened up his food tray.

"You've got to excuse me, Monroe, but I'm hungry bro," Turner said. He tore into a piece of chicken. "You want some of this jerk chicken? There's more than enough. Got some red beans and rice, cabbage too."

"No thanks. I'm all jerked out. Seems like that's all everybody eat is jerk chicken. Fuck, I mean forget all that, Turner. You'll put in a good word for me with Tamara? Hold on, damn, I'm jumpin' the gun, is she married or with somebody?"

Turner deposited a clean chicken bone into his food tray. "No, sir. She's not seeing anyone."

"Alright, then hook yo' boy up, Turner."

"Depends."

"On what, Turner?"

Turner sat back in his chair. "Like I said, it depends. It depends on what you on. I would never tell her, that's something you'll have to do, but I know your background. Tamara's a good girl, not as naïve as she seems, but naïve nonetheless. She's single and a romantic. She's a dreamer and impressionable, so I have to watch out for her. We need her kind around, she's valuable and I don't want to let no man destroy her, especially if I can help it."

"Wow," Roe remarked in disbelief. "Did you just say that I'm going to destroy her?"

"You wondering how I can say something like that Monroe? Because it ain't no stretch of imagination. These young girls get caught up in y'all gangsta lifestyles every day. They end up taking cases for bangers, getting caught in drug conspiracies and get killed by the opps. Every damn day."

"I ain't even goin' hard like that Turner. I'm movin' a little weed, honestly, but I ain't touchin' the hard stuff. I been down that path. Family is Family, but I ain't out here banging. I ain't into it with nobody and I ain't got no opps. I want to do some other shit, though I just don't know where to start. I got a degree in business management and a certificate in food prep in the joint. I even wrote a business plan."

Turner paused with a forkful of cabbage on the way to his mouth. His interest had obviously been piqued because he asked, "A business plan for what?"

"For a café specializing in breakfast and lunch sandwiches."

Turner wiped his hands and mouth with a napkin and closed the food tray. He picked up his ginger beer and sat back in his chair. "I can help you get that going, Monroe. I can get you a storefront, easy. Near somewhere with plenty of foot traffic like the new police station. What's your credit look like?"

"I ain't never had none," Roe admitted. "Never needed none. I always lived by C.R.E.A.M."

"C.R.E.A.M.? What's that?" Turner asked with a puzzled look on his face.

"Cash ruled everything around me," Roe responded.

"Well, that was then, this is now," Turner said. He picked up a pen and pad and jotted down a few notes. "The first thing we gotta do is get you some credit, make you look like something on paper. There's a sister I work with that works miracles with credit. She's 100% legit though and fast. She'll have you looking good in no time at all. You'll just have to do whatever she tells you to. To run any business, you're going to need purchasing power and this'll do it. It should run like $1,000, maybe $1,200 total, but she'll take it in portions."

"Let's do it," Roe said. Standing up, Roe took out his bankroll and quickly counted out $1,200. He put it on the desk in front of Turner and started to leave.

"Where you going?" Turner asked, picking up the money and putting it under the clip on one of the clipboards on his desk.

"Shid, I was finta be out," Roe replied. "There go the cash."

Turner pointed towards the chair, Roe had just vacated. "No sir, Mr. Monroe, have a seat sir. You've got to learn the process. I gotta get an intake done on you. It's just basic information, then I'll get you a receipt for your cash. Then you can be on your way, with Tamara's business card in your pocket."

Roe took his seat again, knowing for Tamara's contact information, he would willingly fill out a million forms.

CHAPTER TWENTY-EIGHT

After maneuvering around a double parked car, Roe mostly pulled into a parking space at the park. He cut his vehicle off and got out of it. "Yo', Family, let me get some help," he yelled to a couple of the guys standing around. Two of the three men walked over to him as Roe lifted the rear door of his Mazda SUV.

"Man, project niggas know they can't park," one of the men joked as he neared the vehicle. "None of our asses can."

"Shid, we parked the way we wanted to back in the days," Roe said with a laugh.

"What you need though, big homie?" the other man asked.

"Help me with these waters and pops and shit," Roe answered. "We takin' them right there by the grill and sit 'em on the picnic tables. Aye shorty, grab that bread and chips off the seat."

The boy he was talking to, stopped, dropped his basketball and went to the car to get the bags. Meanwhile, Roe and the rest of his help carried the cases of pop and water over to the picnic tables.

"Want me to slam your hatchback for you?" one of the guys asked.

"Nall, I got it," Roe said. He pushed a button on the car alarm fob and the door lowered itself.

"Roe! Whaddup, Family," his friend named Bobbo yelled from where he was stationed at the barbecue grill.

"Bobbo, my nigga, waddup Family," Roe called back. He had always loved the homie Bobbo, and it was evident in his smile as he strode over to his friend. He wanted to hug his friend, but the big guy damn near stiff-armed him.

"Watch out, nigga, you see I'm greasy and smoky, ain't no tellin' how much that shit you got on cost, and I can't afford to replace it," Bobbo joked.

"Man, get yo' ass outta here," Roe said. He shook Bobbo's hand and gave him a hug. "You got it smellin' good out here, bro. You almost look like you know what you doin'.'"

"Nigga, I got a black belt in this barbecue shit," Bobbo quipped. "I'm like Bruce Lee, but instead of nun-chucks I got tongs."

"Yeah, right. Well, I stopped and grabbed some pops, waters, bread and chips. I hope it's gone be somethin' ready today."

Bobbo opened the humongous grill and flipped some of the meat on it. "Something'll be comin' off soon. But yeah, Family, that nigga Polo was tellin' me how y'all had to straighten one of them little niggas out. That's crazy."

What's crazy is this nigga Polo running his mouth about something like that, Roe thought. He said, "It wasn't personal, nigga broke the rules. You violate, you get violated."

"I know that's right," Bobbo agreed, shaking hands with Roe. "Nall, I just wanted to tell you, hold it down out here my nigga. Don't catch no bodies, Family. You gotta walk light, my nigga. Might have to go get them CDLs or that car dealer license like I did. Ain't nothin' wrong with doin' some different shit, fam. I ain't tryna preach to you or nothin'.'"

"It's cool, Pastor Bobbo," Roe joked. "But nall, I feel you my nigga, this shit is takin' some gettin' used to, I can't lie. I'm used to bein' a certain way and this shit is totally different. I feel like I missed everything, like I wonder how different shit would be if we woulda been still out here in the last days."

"I think you worried about the wrong thing, Family," Bobbo observed. "Because y'all was locked up you thinkin' everything was all good. It wasn't all good, my nigga. If you was here, it was a chance y'all coulda got killed, locked up, lost it all, ended up on crack, a lot of shit coulda happened. Everybody ain't make it through. I lost my brother. A nigga stuck him up, took his chain and shoes and his life. I lost my auntie and my old man to the rock, too. They both livin' but they caused our family so much hurt, they might as well be dead. We all miss the projects, but some of us was downright sick of them, too. I miss a lot of shit about 'em, but not everything."

"Yeah, I think about that too, Bobbo. I mean, I lost my mama to these projects long before she died."

"Yeah, my condolences," Bobbo said. "All I know is, the shit we thought was so cool as gangsta kids, just don't feel the same. Man, I wanna have grandkids one day and I don't want to raise them in a place like we was raised. I think it was the asbestos that made us all crazy. That and the lead paint. Aye, grab a plate, I got some meat ready. Fix you a plate before the rest of these vulture muthafuckas who ain't never got no money on nothin' get to it."

Roe went over to the picnic table and got a plate. He put a couple of pieces of bread on it and walked back to the grill. Bobbo placed several choice ribs, and a delicious looking steak on his plate.

"Don't look now, but here comes yo' boy and his buddy," Bobbo said, nodding his head in the direction of Polo and Joe Perry as they approached.

Roe carried his plate over to a table and took a seat. He dumped some Sweet Baby Ray's barbecue sauce on it and poured some potato chips on his plate. He took a seat and was eating when Polo sat next to him and took a rib off his plate.

Polo took a huge bite off of the rib. "Damn, Bobbo you still got it Family!" he shouted. "Roe, this rib good as hell."

"Waddup, Roe," Joe Perry said.

Without looking up from his plate, Roe said, "Shit."

Undaunted, Joe Perry continued, "That shit do look good, but where is the sides? No potato salad, no baked beans or shit?"

"Maybe you ain't never been to one, but this is a hood barbecue, you get bread and meat. You lucky it's some barbecue sauce."

"I see," Joe Perry said.

"Fuck all that Roe, I need to holla at yo' ass," Polo said, in between bites. "Look Roe, I'm finta…"

Roe looked at Polo, staring daggers at him. "Slow the fuck down, Polo," he warned.

"What, nigga?" Polo asked.

"If you want to holla at me, pull me to the side like a playa,

Family," Roe told him.

Polo forged ahead anyway, he said, "Man, I ain't tryna hear that shit, Family, nigga, I need you to..."

Without so much as a word, Roe stood up, picked up his plate and walked away.

"What's up with yo' boy? He playin' right?" Joe Perry asked.

Polo tossed his rib bone onto the table and stood up also. "I'm finta go see what he on."

Joe Perry made to get up too, he said, "Yeah, let's see what this nigga on."

"Fall back, J.P., I know this nigga. He on that joint, don't trust nobody shit. Just gimme a minute to holla at him. I'll be right back, just let me calm this nigga down."

Roe had walked over to an empty park bench, where he took a seat and was eating.

Polo took a seat on the bench next to him and took some of his chips from his plate. "Fuck wrong with you, Roe? Why you get up and leave like that, nigga?"

"It's like you don't fuckin' get it, Lo!" Roe said, his voice dripping with exasperation. "I keep tellin' you the same shit. Don't say shit to me in front of no nigga! I don't give a fuck who they is. And why the fuck is you tellin' muthafuckas about that move at Antrell crib. Big as yo' mouth is, I'm glad we didn't kill shorty nem."

"Man, yo' ass paranoid as hell, we ain't do shit bogus, we ain't kill them niggas."

"Nigga, yo' ass trippin', that was a home invasion," Roe said. "Whether we did something or not, that shit ain't nobody's business. And quit tryna talk to me in front of that nigga."

"You still trippin' on my man, Joe Perry?"

"That's yo' man, not mine nigga and I ain't finta keep tellin' you that," Roe stated. "I don't know that nigga and don't fuckin' trust him. I don't know none of these niggas when it comes down to my freedom. I fucks with you. You!"

Polo reached for Roe's plate again, but Roe moved it. Polo laughed. "I got you, nigga. Look, when I called you earlier, you was downtown. Fuck you was doing down there?"

"Gettin' my business license shit straight."

"You gettin' a business license to trap, nigga?" Polo joked. "You don't need no license for that."

"I bet you think you sounded funny sayin' that shit. Nall, funny ass nigga, I'm gone open me a restaurant."

"Fuck you know about runnin' a restaurant, Roe?"

"Nigga, I ain't stupid. I got a degree in business. I'm finta make that shit work for me. I got a daughter and I'm trying to make sure she got a future. I don't want her to have to work for nobody, but herself. Fuck all that though, what yo' ass wanted?"

Polo stood up from the bench. "Roe, hear me out. I need 20 gees from you real quick."

"Damn, nigga, what the fuck you tryna do?"

Polo sat back down and put his arm around Roe's shoulders. He said, "I got a crazy deal on some heroin. Plug prices. I can't pass this up, I'm tryna grab the shit tonight. This shit a fuckin' bomb, too. I'll have yo' 20 bucks back in a coupla days at the most, and I can throw you another ten thousand, maybe to invest in the restaurant."

"And this the shit you wanted to ask me in front of a nigga I don't fuck with?" Roe asked incredulously. "Wow! Yo' ass is tweakin'. You better quit fuckin' with that raw. Yo' slip is showin', like Cindy Brady used to say."

"Man, fuck all that, do you got me or what?"

"I ain't got it, got it, but I'm gone give it to you. I want my money back, Lo. This the bread to help open my joint. I'ma need that back, nigga."

Polo sat back and pulled his sunglasses onto his eyes. "Boy, in a couple of days, you gone have that plus ten more. Now can we go over there and get some more of that food before it's all gone."

"Yeah, I want some of them wings," Roe said. He picked up his plate and he and Polo started walking back to the cookout. Roe stopped, to Polo, he said, "When I leave here, I'm gone go get that for you."

"Don't worry bro, I got you. This gone go smooth. I'll be back at you in a coupla days on my life. I'm finta grab three bricks of that shit and I'm off and runnin'. I'm tellin' you, yo' cash is guaranteed. You in good hands with All-State, my nigga. Tomorrow, I'm gone be up and running with that dynamite and you can take that to church. Oh shit, speakin' of church, Family, did you ever get up with Cindy Brady? She told me to tell you get up with her, she got somethin' for you."

Roe started back walking. "I ain't got time for that religious shit, bro. I wanna see my auntie, but I don't want to hear that save my soul shit. The world don't work like that to me. She still doin' good though?"

"Hell yeah, Roe. She look good too. All she do is work and go to church. She might drink a little wine with her church buddies, but that's it. She don't even want to talk about the old days 'less she testifyin'. I'm tellin' you, you need to see her."

"Right now, the only thing I need to see is some of that chicken Bobbo got comin' off that grill," Roe said.

CHAPTER TWENTY-NINE

Roe pulled up to the coffee shop to get his morning cup of joe and play a game or two of chess with his buddy, Bone. Before he could leave the vehicle, his phone buzzed with a text alert. He took his phone from the cup holder and viewed the text.

Tamara: runnin late from being on the phone all nite with a certain someone

Roe was smiling as he typed: that was u. I was tryin 2 go 2 bed

Tamara: stop it

Roe: all jokes aside I really like talkin 2 u

Tamara: likewise have a good day king

Roe: u 2 Queen call u later?

Tamara: 4 sho

He was still grinning as he pushed the door open of the café. As he walked to the counter to place his order, he nodded at Bone, who returned his nod. Oddly, he noticed Bone's chess set was missing for the first time since he'd been coming here for over a year.

"Medium coffee, four sugars, four creams and a banana nut muffin," he ordered. Over his shoulder, he asked, "What you want this a.m., big bro? No chess?"

"I'm good over here, God," he answered. "It's too many hyenas in the jungle for this old lion. I don't feel like playing the game of kings with all these extra pawns on the board."

Bone's remarks didn't fall on deaf ears and Roe inconspicuously used the mirrors on the walls to take a look around the room. Immediately he noticed four people that didn't belong there; a white man and woman at one table and two men, one white and one black at another. They were all trying to look like they belonged and that fact made them look the total opposite. As Roe paid for his order, the men and the woman all stood. Roe tucked his change in his pocket and put his hands in the air. One of the men whipped out a badge on his neck chain and a gun materialized in his hand.

"D.E.A., Monroe Pearson," he announced.

His hands remained in the air, as he said, "My name is Monroe Pearson. My Illinois state driver's license is in my pocket in my wallet, and I'm invoking my right to counsel and to remain silent."

The agents all came forward, handcuffed Roe and took him into custody. They escorted him from the café and put him in their car. As the car containing Roe drove away, Bone held up a fist salute, which Roe acknowledged with a head nod.

....

Sitting at the table in the interview room in the Drug Enforcement Agency suite at the Dirksen Federal Building in downtown Chicago, Roe can't stop shaking his head as he looked around. The door to the room he was in opened up and in walked Joe Perry. His D.E.A. ID badge hung from a chain around his neck. Surprise registered on Roe's face for a few seconds, but he swiftly recovered. Joe Perry placed a cup of coffee and a donut on the table in front of him and took a seat across from him.

"Might not be as good as the café's coffee and pastry," Joe Perry said.

Roe took a sip. "It'll do."

They stared at one another for a moment, mentally circling one another like opponents in a boxing match.

"How did you know?" Joe Perry asked.

"I just came home from prison, I know when a nigga ain't right."

"C'mon Roe, you gotta admit that my act was good. I got your man, Polo."

"I don't know nothin' about that," Roe said. He took a bite of the donut, but he really didn't have an appetite.

"Oh yeah, I did get him," Joe Perry said smugly. "You

though, you're pretty smart. Too smart for your own good really. You fuck around, but nothing too heavy. I know about the little weed you movin', but I'll be damned if I have some baby ass weed bust in my jacket. If you woulda been on parole, I would have sent you back inside though."

Roe shrugged and sipped his coffee. "Do what you gotta do dog, but I ain't got shit to say about shit. I want it on the record that you're violating my rights by interrogating me without an attorney present."

Joe Perry laughed. "I'm not interrogating you, I'm just talking with you. There was a couple of times I thought I had you, but you wiggled out of it. They were actually trying to find something to charge you with, but I had to keep it a 100 and let them know you weren't selling heroin, which was actually our focus. My superiors don't give you credit though, they think if given time, you'll end up in Polo's shoes. I don't think so though."

"So, if you know I ain't got shit to do with nothin', then why you pull me in here?" Roe asked.

Joe Perry sat forward in his chair. "Because I did have a question. Polo was short on the money for the three keys of dope. He came to talk to you, and suddenly he had the rest of the money. You do know if you gave him that money, then you would be charged as his co-conspirator. You gave him that money, didn't you?"

Roe folded his arms and sat back in his chair. "I ain't gave nobody shit, homie. I don't know what you talkin' about."

"Yeah, so what did he talk to you about at that cookout?"

"My nigga had bitch problems," Roe said innocently. "You know how that shit go. Fuck all that though, how it look for my man?"

"I'm not sorry to say he's fucked," Joe Perry admitted. "It's pretty bad. He just bought three kilos of heroin from us last night, plus all the stuff we already had on him. Like I said, it's pretty bad."

"You really sound like you enjoy jammin' a nigga up, Black man," Roe said disgustedly. "Joe Perry, I know that not yo' name, you kicked it with that man every day. Y'all fucked bitches together, snorted coke and got drunk together, y'all broke bread almost every day. How you sleep at night, knowing you takin' down yo' own kind for the master?"

"Get the fuck outta here with that bullshit," Joe Perry said. "I sleep as easy as men like Polo do when they know they're selling poison to our people. Remember this, Monroe, we don't go after innocent men. We're not CPD, guessing our way into cases. If we're on you, it's because we already know what we know. If you're not breaking the law, you don't have to worry about us. We don't bother you. It's simple, if you don't want to go to prison, then don't sell drugs. Now like I said, I only wanted to ask you a question and since you've cleared things up for me, you're free to go. You want us to drop you somewhere?"

Roe didn't even dignify that remark with an answer as he got up and left. Joe Perry spun around in his chair a couple of times, and then left the room too.

CHAPTER THIRTY

"Alright, baby girl, I'll pick you up from school today," Roe said into his cell phone. "Have a good day, M, I'll see you later."

He dropped the phone on the bed and lay there looking at the ceiling. He got a text alert and picked up his phone. It was from Tamara.

Tamara: Hope u're feeling better Call when u're ready

Roe: Thanks Will do

He dropped his phone on the bed again. His trap phone rang. He started to ignore it, but then decided to answer it.

"Yeah, Rio. I'll get at you this morning. I got you lil' homie." He ended that call and tossed his trap phone onto the bed. As he lay there, all he could think about was his friend, Polo's plight. He knew his homie would more than likely be going to prison for the rest of his life. His crew, the original Family Members had taken some hard hits, and now Polo was back in MCC downtown with a heavy case.

Things were so heavy on his mind; Roe went to talk to Turner. He found that he liked talking to the older, Black man. He was wise in both street and real world matters and it was turning out his counsel was invaluable. Even when he told Turner he'd given Polo his startup capital for his restaurant, Turner was undaunted. "That's why we're fixing your credit," is all he said. "May take longer, but that'll only make you stronger."

That didn't make him feel much better. It was depressing thinking about how everything was so much different now, and it felt like the world didn't care. He had grown to like talking to Tamara, and was doing so daily, but even her soft voice and beautiful smile couldn't cheer him up right now. He did see a future with her, though. He liked the fact she was different from all of the women he'd dated before. He had decided that he had some more hoeing to do, but settling down one day was becoming a more and more attractive idea; especially with a woman like Tamara. He had once heard Bobbo say that he loved his wife because she didn't take his shit, and she brought him peace. Maybe he was being fooled, but he thought he already saw those types of qualities in Tamara. Just the thought of her soft voice and intelligent conversation brought him a good feeling. He was already thinking those characteristics were something that would be hard to fake, but he would wait and see.

There was a knock at his room door. "Money Roe, you decent?" his aunt Martha asked.

Roe sat up and swung his legs off the bed. "Yeah, Auntie. I'm decent."

Martha opened the door and looked in the room. "Hey Money, just had to tell you that I'm on my way to work, and Cindy Brady is in the living room waiting on you. Ok, see you later."

She tried to close the door, but Roe held up his hand. "Wait. Wait. Wait. Auntie, you didn't say what I think you said. You didn't say that. You wouldn't do that to your nephew and your birthday is less than a month away."

"What?" his aunt asked innocently. "My sister wanted to see you, she misses her nephew too. She's popped by a few times but she keeps missing you. I just happened to mention that you were a bit down because of what happened to Polo."

Roe fell backward on the bed and covered his face with his hands. "Auntie, I can't believe you played me like that. You know I don't want to hear all that religious crap. I don't believe in none of it. She ain't finta be baptizing me in alkaline water or whatever she was tryna tell me when I was locked up."

Martha laughed. "Money, you stupid. I'm sure she ain't finta do all that. Plus, who don't need some prayer and to be baptized these days. Get up and see yo' auntie, boy. She say she got somethin' for you. I'm gone."

"It's probably like a 40-ounce of Jesus sweat or something," Roe pouted. He pulled his pillow over his head for a moment, then cast it aside and got out of bed. He put his Adidas slides on and went to the living room.

In the living room, Cindy Brady was looking at the framed family pictures on the wall. She was much heavier than she was back in her days as a rock star, though she still wore blonde hair, it wasn't in pigtails.

"Cindy Brady, what is you doin' wakin' me up early in the mornin'?" Roe asked.

When she turned and saw him, she squealed and rushed over to him. They both hugged one another tightly and Roe had to admit to himself that he'd missed his Aunt Cindy, very much so. He also realized why he hadn't been in a rush to see her—she looked just like his mother. After a few moments, they broke apart.

Unsure of what to do, Roe said, "Auntie, I'm about to get me a bottle of water. You want one?"

"I'll take one, Money Roe" Cindy Brady said. "You know why we call you Money Roe, right?"

"Yeah, Auntie, I know the story."

"Yeah, your cousin couldn't pronounce Monroe, so she called you Money Roe," Cindy Brady informed him anyway.

In the kitchen, Roe took two bottles of water from the fridge and returned to the living room. Cindy Brady had taken a seat on the couch, so he joined her.

"You lookin' good, Auntie. I'm glad to see that."

Cindy Brady smoothed her slacks. "Yeah, I did the crackhead thing already, I had enough of that role. It was time for somethin' else. Now, I'm a child of God, blessed and highly favored. The Bible says..."

"Cindy Brady, later for Bible study. What is it that you had to give me?"

She took a manila envelope from her bag on the floor beside the couch and handed it to Roe. He looked in the envelope and to his surprise it was filled with money. Roe looked up from the contents to his aunt with a questioning look on his face.

"Where did you get this money, Cindy Brady? And why are you giving it to me? You aren't like the Bible Verse Bank Robber or somethin'?"

His aunt laughed, "Stop playin', Money. That ain't from me, that's from your cousin Terrell."

Roe pulled some of the stacks of cash from the envelope and examined them to see if it was real. "And he gave it to you to give to me? I live with his mother."

"Don't say it like that Money. Terrell knew I was gone give you yo' money. Every cent of it. Plus, he knew that he couldn't get it back from me. His mama though, Martha would have gave it back if he whined enough; me, I'm not goin'. You said don't give it back to you, I'm not giving it back to you. It's all there, $20,000."

"So you mean to tell me that you've been holdin' this for me, for a couple of years now?"

Cindy Brady twisted the cap off of her bottled water. She was about to tip the bottle to pour some out for her dead homies, when she caught herself and laughed a bit. She said, "Old habits die hard, I just almost poured out some for my niggas that ain't here. Sweet Jesus. Yeah, well about the cash, we didn't know it was gonna take you so long to get out. Terrell just wanted to make sure you came home to something. He was making a lot of money so he wanted you to be straight. I been tryna catch up with you since you came home, so this is yo' fault it took so long to get to you."

They talked for another half hour or so, but Roe was distracted because his mind kept wandering back to the cash his cousin had left him. He decided that the moment the office of Community Development Inc. opened this morning, he would be there letting Turner know to go ahead full steam; it was definitely time.

Cindy Brady broke through his thoughts, when she announced, "Money, I got to get to work. Give your auntie one more hug so I can be on my way. Remember nephew, not everybody gets a second chance. We did though and I'm goin' to make mine count. You ain't got to let go of the past, it can actually make you a better person if you learn from your mistakes. Just promise me you won't be afraid to take yo' shot."

"I won't Auntie, not no more," Roe said as he came forward to hug her.

As they hugged, Cindy Brady said, "And call me one Sunday so we can get over to the church and catch a sermon together. Pastor be screamin' on these wannabe saints and these hypocritical church folk."

"I'll do that," Roe said, his voice loaded with sarcasm. He walked her to the door and said his goodbyes. The moment the door was locked behind her, he dashed to his bedroom to get his phone. He took a seat and pulled the envelope onto his lap as he waited for his call to connect. It went to Turner's voicemail.

"Turn Up, this is Roe. I want that storefront they showed me last week if it's still available. The one by the police station, next to that beauty supply and salon. Tell the landlord I can live with the two-month buildout, too. Let me know so I can get the money orders. No matter what though, I'm going to the restaurant supply store to start buyin' the equipment…"

As he was leaving the voicemail, Turner called on the other line. Roe clicked over, "Turn Up, I was just leavin' you a message. Aye, big bro, I need…"

CHAPTER THIRTY-ONE

Malika walked into M & M's Sandwich Shack, their new breakfast and lunch restaurant. It was still under construction, but there wasn't that much to be done and it had really taken shape. Roe was on a ladder straightening the large menu sign the workers had already installed.

"A little to the left," Malika said.

He adjusted the sign and looked over at his daughter. She signaled for him to move it a little more—he did. He looked back at her. She cocked her head to the side at first, and then gave him the thumbs up.

"That's it right there, Pops," she said with a huge grin. "You got my spot looking good!"

"Our spot," Roe corrected her as he descended the ladder. He walked over and put his arm around her shoulders as they both looked up at the sign with pride.

"You like the sign? It's good right? What do you think about the decorations? Do we need more or less? You gone go on social media, right? You not gone forget to go on social media, are you?"

Malika lightly punched her father in the stomach. "Chill out, Pops. We good over this way. I'm proud of you! You did your thing up in here. I'm gonna take care of the social media. Everything is gonna be good, but you gotta relax though."

Roe took a deep breath. "I'm calm, I'm calm. You just make sure you stay on social media posting shit every day all day. I'll do everything else, but I can't deal with that shit every day. One of them haters will be done said somethin' slick about our food or service or somethin' and I'll be ridin' around lookin' for they ass. Hop out with a big pistol, like now what you say about them sammiches at M & M's?"

They both laughed. Malika said, "Yeah, Pops, we don't need you sliding doing the most, tryna hurt somebody because they ain't get they onion rings with they order."

Her comment brought further laughter. Just then, Rio came through the back door of the restaurant carrying several chairs in which he brought to the dining area. When he saw Malika, he started grinning. He was so preoccupied with her, he would have stepped into a half full paint tray if Roe didn't grab his shirt and steer him away from it.

"Where you want these?" Rio asked. His face reddened slightly from embarrassment.

"Line them up in the front there," Roe said. "I'll help you get the rest of them."

"Me too," Malika offered, a little too eagerly.

Roe looked at her.

"I'll hold the door," she said, avoiding her father's glare.

Shaking his head, Roe led them out of the back door to get the rest of the chairs from the back of Roe's SUV. Together, Roe and Rio moved several sets of chairs inside while Malika held the door and made goo-goo eyes at Rio. As they were arranging the table and chairs in the dining area, Roe's got a text.

Tamara: u at M&Ms?

Roe: Yeah We n the café

Tamara: we?

Roe: Me, my daughter and the first employee I'm gonna have 2 fire

Tamara: wanted 2 c if u want lunch but u busy

Roe: neva 2 busy 4 u

Tamara: u hungry?

Roe: now that u mention it

Tamara: kids hungry?

Roe: kidz r always hungry

Tamara: burgers, pizza or chicken?

Roe: bird

Tamara: neva met your daughter is it ok?

Roe paused for a second, then he texted: no time like the present C'mon woman b4 I get hangry

Tamara: omw

Roe knew it was a first, but he definitely felt like it was a step in the right direction. He knew the day was fast approaching as he and Tamara had grown closer in the last two and half months. He looked over at his daughter and Rio. They were standing close to one another looking at a video on one of their phones.

"Aye!" he barked, startling them both, almost causing Rio to drop his phone, but he recovered before it hit the floor. "There's some lunch on the way, but we can still do some work. Lika, start stocking the drink coolers. Rio, you follow me, we gotta get the rest of this water and pop out of the back and bring them up front."

In the next half hour, they worked up a sweat as they completed several tasks. Roe was wiping his hands on a shop rag when Tamara walked in the restaurant carrying two huge bags of fried chicken and side orders. Roe took the bags from her and gave her a peck on the lips. He put the bags on the table.

"Malika and Rio, this is Tamara," Roe pronounced. "Tamara, Malika and soon to be fired Rio."

When they came forward, Tamara hugged both of them. Malika turned to her father and nodded her approval. She winked at him.

"I see the place is coming along nicely, Monroe," Tamara said looking around. "You've got a lot done in the last two weeks. I like the look, too. Clean, simple and functional. Good job!"

"Thank you, Tamara. We're actually ahead of schedule. So early in fact, we can have a soft opening and a grand opening. As early as Monday, I'll be interviewing for cooks and staff."

Malika cleared her throat several times.

"I mean we will be interviewing cooks and staff," Roe corrected himself.

"That's better," Malika said.

"Alright, alright, let's eat," Roe said. He led the way over to the table and they all seated themselves.

Tamara started opening the bags of food. She said, "I didn't know what everybody eats, so I just got some of everything. Don't be shy, everybody dig in."

They all began to fill their plates, and soon their bellies. They talked and laughed amongst themselves and Roe could see Malika and Tamara would easily get along. Rio was just happy to be anywhere Malika was. Malika took a few selfies of them all and posted them on the Sandwich Shop's Instagram and Facebook pages.

Roe pushed his chair back from the table. He got up and went to the coolers. "What you guys want to drink?" he asked. "The only thing cold is water." He opened the sliding door of one of the coolers and got a bottle for himself.

Malika answered first. "Water for me and Rio. Tamara what would you like?"

"Water's fine," she answered. "Tell me you see some jalapeno poppers in one of them bags."

"Oh snap, now I know I likes you!" Malika declared.

Tamara laughed. She asked, "Now, what makes you say that?"

"Well, besides me, you're the only person that makes my Pops smile for real, and you like jalapeno poppers," Malika answered matter-of-factly as she searched through the bags. She held up a smaller bag containing the poppers. "Bingo."

As Roe watched their interaction, he had to admit for one of the few times since he could remember in his life, he was actually happy. He turned back to the cooler to get water for the rest of them. Four teens wearing school uniforms and backpacks, pushed the restaurant door open and came inside.

"Y'all open?" one of the high school students asked.

"Not yet, youngin', in about a week though we'll be ready," Roe said. He walked over and put the water bottles on the table where they were eating. He went over to the kids and shook their hands. "Y'all come back Monday after next and the doors will be open for breakfast and lunch. Stop through next week, we'll have coupons printed up for y'all. Take a few flyers and let your friends know."

The kids examined the flyers. They seemed excited. The girl with them said, "I can't wait to try this four cheese grilled cheese with grilled avocados. We go to school right down the street, we finta be in here all the time."

"I want this pot roast sandwich," another teen said.

"Well, I'm on these breakfast sandwiches, egg, bacon and

hash brown on French toast. That sounds so good," the first teen said. "We'll be back, y'all. Thanks."

The teens left out of the door chattering and talking about the new restaurant. Roe went to lock the door behind him, and he couldn't even hide the huge grin on his face when he turned back to Malika, Tamara and Rio.

He went to the table and put his arm around Malika and Tamara. "I think we got somethin' here y'all. I think we got somethin'. I think we got somethin'."

"Yeah, we do. We got something, Pops," Malika reassured him.

Roe hugged her and Tamara tight. Rio came around the table to join them in a group hug by hugging Malika, but a look from Roe shut him down. He went and sat back down. Releasing them, Roe kissed Malika on the forehead and Tamara on the cheek. He went and took his seat.

"Now pass me some of them smashed potatoes and some chicken thighs," Roe said.

....

Eighteen months later, Roe stood at the podium at a Young Entrepreneurs banquet sponsored by Turner and his Community Development organization. He had just been introduced as a keynote speaker by the vice mayor of Chicago. He looked out in the audience at all of the boys and girls, young men and women, dressed in business attire. They looked really good. The positive energy and hope flowing from them was amazing. All of their eyes were trained on him as he stood there holding his index cards with talking points on them.

He fidgeted a bit because the collar of his dress shirt was bothering him a bit and he didn't like his necktie. He made a mental note to go shopping for some better ties. Tamara had told him not to wear that one. He looked over his shoulder at his wife-to-be Tamara, sitting on the stage behind him with her legs primly crossed. She mouthed, "You got this." He mouthed back, "Yeah, I do."

He turned back to the audience and cleared his throat. "My name is Monroe Pearson, and I'm getting a chance to do something many of the people I grew up with didn't get a chance to do. I'm getting a chance to follow my dreams.

Growing up in the projects, one of the first things to die is your dreams. It seems like at times friends and family go out of their way to crush your hopes because their hopes have been crushed. You learn to stop thinking about tomorrow just so you can make it through today."

"It took a wild ride for me to get where I am today and I've lost too much to count, but always remember losses make bosses. Sometimes what you think is the end, is merely the beginning, but you have to know, in order to change your life or circumstances the first thing you have to change is your mind. The place I grew up in and loved so much doesn't exist anymore, and that was really hard for me to wrap my mind around. That fact had me depressed and feeling like I'd lost the race before I ever started. Like many people that were displaced by the housing developments they knew and loved being torn down, I'll always miss it, but you have to be able to adapt to new circumstances."

It's okay to grow beyond what you once were, and become what you always wanted to be. A little over a year ago, I was afraid to open my bistro and now I'm ready to open my second, with plans for my third one in the works. None of this would have been possible if I wasn't forced out of my comfort zone. So, now here stands an ex-hustler, slash dope boy, slash ex-convict to now a proud business owner that employs others and has a bright future. Believe me, if I can do it, you can too. I don't wish you all good luck, I wish that you are all prepared when the opportunity presents itself."

At the end of his speech, Roe stood there for a moment at the podium. The room was totally silent for a few seconds before people began springing to their feet. They rewarded Roe's honesty with a standing ovation that lasted for two solid minutes. With tears in his eyes he made his way over to Tamara and Malika. He hugged his daughter first and then gave his woman a long, strong hug. As he turned to face the audience to smile and wave at them, he tucked his hand into his suit jacket pocket and fingered the engagement ring box. He looked across the stage and winked at Turner, who nodded his head knowingly.

ACKNOWLEDGMENT

To my children: Cacharel, Ciara and Yanier. I love you all more than you'll ever know. Each of your lights have helped to illuminate the darkness around me at different times. Blessings to you each.

To Jami Rhue, thanks for being there and being dope. You have my extreme gratitude for letting me borrow your strength and positive energy on many occasions. Your hugs are like a charger for the soul. Blessings.

To my brother, the Ghost Rider aka Rat, aka Scuddy. Damn Ghost, you are missed, bro. Your loyalty, heart and hustle made you legendary, my Negro. I'm hurting personally, but I know there's a huge hole in many people's lives because of your absence. Your family, your mother (Rivian Coker), your sisters (Berkenya and Vivian), twin daughters (Shaniyah and Taniyah), father and brother (Willie and Theotis), nephews, nieces, cousins, your lady (Meka), and your homies all over (Extensions, Ida B. Wells, 39TH Street, South C), are all hurting, bro. You would always say that I saved your life in more ways than one, but best believe my homie the feeling is mutual, you saved mine more times than I can count. I'm gonna miss you forever, my homie. Peace to a really dope soul. Word

Willie "Rat" Coker aka Ghost Rider aka Scuddy

11/24/1976 – 08/31/2019

NIGHT TIME BLUES

I'll see your face in those that came before and after you

I'll hear you in their laughter too

I'll think of you anytime I see dominoes on a card table

For me this is a hard fable

But this story has to be told

How you ain't gone grow old?

Limping around, feeding cats, spitting gangster-isms

Full of common sense & wisdom

I'd give anything to see you grin your lopsided grin again my friend

And it's almost a sin how much of a twin you were to your twins

In your time here you'd been thru a lot

Been hit by cars and shot

Locked and freed

You loved to hustle but despised greed

If he called you friend he would be there when you were in need

Though maybe not with speed

Because you most assuredly moved at your own pace

With the project's precision and the ghetto's grace

King among kings

A man among men

A friend among friends

Your word was your bond, what you said you did

Everyone knows you loved you some little kids

A man of many names

But everyone loved you the same

This is already a cold world

And now without you here it's freezing

There's no believing that you'd be leaving in such an early season without reason

You meant many things to each & every one of us

Many words describe your character like honor, respect, loyalty & trust

You wanted to win at everything and wanted to play again if you lost

But you weren't a cheater and didn't try to win at any cost

You've joined the stars in the sky and in this darkness we need your light

Maybe some of us will feel better if we know you look down on us every night

Hopefully you'll shine extra bright to let us know you're alright

Peace dear friend, brother, and father

www.ingramcontent.com/pod-product-compliance
Lightning Source LLC
Chambersburg PA
CBHW072123170626
46813CB00004B/1674